THIS BOOK
BELONGS TO

- - - - - - - - - - - - - -

- - - - - - - - - - -

BY THE SAME AUTHOR

SELBY
SHATTERED

DUNCAN BALL

with illustrations by Allan Stomann

Angus&Robertson
An imprint of HarperCollins*Publishers*

Angus&Robertson
An imprint of HarperCollins*Publishers*, Australia

First published in Australia in 2006
by HarperCollins*Publishers* Australia Pty Limited
ABN 36 009 913 517
www.harpercollins.com.au

Text © Duncan Ball 2006
Illustrations copyright © Allan Stomann 2006

The right of Duncan Ball and Allan Stomann to be identified as the author and
illustrator of this work has been asserted by them in accordance with the *Copyright
Amendment (Moral Rights) Act 2000.*

HarperCollins*Publishers*
25 Ryde Road, Pymble, Sydney, NSW 2073, Australia
31 View Road, Glenfield, Auckland 10, New Zealand
77–85 Fulham Palace Road, London W6 8JB, United Kingdom
2 Bloor Street East, 20th floor, Toronto, Ontario M4W 1A8, Canada
10 East 53rd Street, New York NY 10022, USA

National Library of Australia Cataloguing-in-Publication data:

Ball, Duncan, 1941– .
  Selby shattered.
  For children aged 8–12 years.
  ISBN 13: 978 0 2072 0066 3 (pbk).
  ISBN 10: 0 2072 0066 1 (pbk).
  1. Dogs – Juvenile literature. I. Stomann, Allan. II. Title.
A823.3

Cover concept by Christa Moffitt, Christabella Designs
Cover design by Matt Stanton
Cover and internal illustrations by Allan Stomann
Typeset in 14/18 Bembo by Helen Beard, ECJ Australia Pty Limited
Printed and bound in Australia by Griffin Press on 60gsm Bulky Paperback

6 5 4 3   07 08 09

This book is dedicated to you.

It's not for your sister or your brother or your parents, your teacher or even your best friend. It's only for you and no one else.

AUTHOR'S NOTE

Selby is not just the only talking dog in Australia and, perhaps, the world but he's also the only dog in the world who has had nine lives. More than nine lives. I've lost count of the number of times Selby should have died but managed to survive against all odds.

As the readers of these books will know, Selby rings me up and tells me his stories and I just write them down. But when he rang a while ago to tell me about his most recent adventures, I have to admit that I began to doubt him. Hour after hour, I listened spellbound as Selby told me about his most horrible, frightening (but sometimes funny) stories ever. How could a dog survive all these things? Read this book and you'll see!

Duncan Ball

CONTENTS

TOP

I have a terrible feeling that my peaceful life with the Trifles is about to be shattered. Why do I say this? **TOP** of the list is a group called The Search for Selby Society. They want to find me and tell everybody my secret —that I'm the only talking dog in Australia and, perhaps, the world.

And they're not my only worry. By the time you finish reading these tales of action, adventure and romance-gone-wrong (yes, romance!), you'll see why I feel like I'm at the **top** of a rollercoaster about to take off.

Anyway, start at the **top** (which means the beginning) and by the time you get to the end I hope you think that these are **top** tales.

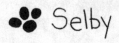 Selby

SELBY CASTAWAY

'Remind me,' Dr Trifle said. 'What did we win and how did we win it?'

'Remember the competition that was in the newspaper about finding a symbol for a new computer company?' Mrs Trifle said.

'Oh, yes. I think you read it out to me.'

'Well, the name of the company is DogsBody Computer Systems and you must have sent in a photo of Selby. They loved it and you won.'

'That's funny, because I don't remember sending anything in.'

'There's a good reason for that,' Selby thought, as he trotted along beside the Trifles. 'Because *you* didn't send it in — *I* did.'

The Trifles and Selby were in the city looking for the office of DogsBody Computer Systems.

'Here it is,' Mrs Trifle said.

She led Dr Trifle and Selby into a big office building. They got into a lift and went down to the floor below.

'Who would name their company after a dead dog?' Dr Trifle asked.

'It's not named after a dead dog. A *dogsbody* is sort of a servant. It's someone who does all those things that you don't want to do.'

'Wouldn't it be great to have your own personal dogsbody?' Dr Trifle said. 'If Selby knew how to talk, he could be our dogsbody and do all the things we don't want to do.'

'Which is why nobody is ever going to find out my secret,' Selby thought. 'I may have a dog's *body* but I'm never going to be a *dogsbody*.'

Finally they arrived at a door that said:

DogsBody Computer Systems
Our computers do the work so you can play
Just send your brain on holiday

Inside was an open-plan office with three men and a woman sitting in front of their computers all wearing little headsets.

'I don't think I could work here,' Mrs Trifle whispered to her husband. 'There are no windows. You wouldn't know if it's raining or sunny or even day or night.'

'Computer people live to work,' Dr Trifle said. 'They're too busy to look out windows. And night and day mean nothing to them. They work all the time.'

'That sounds awful,' Selby thought. 'Work is bad enough, but working all the time would be horrible.'

'Hello,' Dr Trifle sang out.

'They can't hear you,' Mrs Trifle said. 'They're all listening to their little music-player thingies.'

Mrs Trifle waved her hand in front of one of the men's eyes. He quickly pulled off his headset.

'Could you tell me where Mr Zak is?' she asked.

'Hey, guys, I'm Zak. You must be the Trifles. And this must be the famous Selby. Hiya, Sel. Thanks for coming. I'm the boss here at DogsBody Computer Systems.'

'Pleased to meet you,' said Mrs Trifle.

'Hey, dudes!' Zak screamed. 'Come and meet Selby and the Trifles! That's Jason. We call him "the Wizard". Eva is "the Genius" and Miles is "the Mastermind". I call myself Top Dog. Get it? The top dog at DogsBody Computer Systems?'

Jason, Eva and Miles huddled around Selby and patted him while Zak took lots of pictures.

'Selby's really neat!' Eva said. 'Put the glasses on him like in the photo.'

'Glasses?' Dr Trifle said. 'Was he wearing glasses?'

'Yes, and they looked just like yours,' Jason said, taking Dr Trifle's glasses and putting them on Selby. 'There. Just like in the photo you sent us. He looks sort of . . . well, I think *intelligent* is the right word.'

'If it's not, it'll do,' Selby thought as he turned his head this way and that while Zak took more photos.

Snap snap snap.

'We're going to use Selby's face in all our ads,' Eva explained. 'Oh, and here's your prize.'

'Goodness me,' Mrs Trifle said, opening the little box Eva handed her. 'What is it? Why, it's a . . . a . . . a . . . what is it?'

'It's one of our computers,' Zak said. 'We call it TINY.'

'Oh, I get it,' Dr Trifle said with a laugh. 'T-I-N-Y must stand for Techno Integrated Nano Yielder.'

'No,' Zak said. 'We just called it TINY because it's small. It may be small but it'll do anything you want it to. You'll love it.'

'Thank you very much,' Mrs Trifle said.

'Psst!' Eva said. 'Tell them about the SOS.'

'Oh, yes, I completely forgot. Would you mind if Selby came along on the Shore Ocean Shore Yacht Race with us? Now that he's the symbol of DogsBody, we'd love to have him on board. It'll be great publicity for us.'

'A yacht race?' thought Selby. 'I'm not really a sailing sort of dog.'

'A yacht race?' Mrs Trifle said. 'Yes, I'm sure he'd love it.'

'Good. It starts tomorrow and finishes in a couple of days — maybe a week.'

'*Sheeesh!*' Selby thought. 'A couple of days — maybe a week. I don't know about this.'

And so it was that Selby found himself on board the *Sleek Geek*, the newest, longest, most modern yacht in the world.

Selby sat on the deck with the DogsBody people while Dr and Mrs Trifle stood nearby on the pier.

'They don't really seem like sailors to me,' Mrs Trifle said to her husband.

'Why do you say that?'

'Because all the other yachts are out in the harbour at the starting line while the DogsBody people are listening to music and playing with their laptops. Oh, Zak!'

'Yes, Mrs T?'

'Shouldn't you be getting ready for the race?'

'We don't have to do anything,' Zak said. 'TINY is programmed to do everything. When it hears the starting gun, it'll turn on the motors. Then the motors will pull up those big pieces of cloth.'

'Do you mean the *sails*?'

'That's right. Then the computer will measure how fast the air is moving.'

'Do you mean the wind speed?'

'Yes, and it points the boat in the right direction.'

'You mean it *steers* it.'

'I think that's the word, and it pulls the strings that move the big stick back and forth.'

'You mean the *boom*,' Dr Trifle said.

'The boom? No, it starts the motors when it *hears* the boom,' Zak said. 'The computer does absolutely everything. There are cameras that tell the computer how much the water goes up and down, and about the weather — everything.'

'Are you sure you're all going to be okay?' Mrs Trifle asked.

'Don't you worry about us, Mrs T. We've got stacks of computer games. We won't be bored for a minute.'

Just then the starting gun fired and the computer blinked and the sails shot up.

'Hey! There's a picture of me on the sail!' Selby thought. 'And it's gi-*normous*! I am sooooo famous!'

The wind filled the sails and the yacht pulled slowly away from the pier. Then it came to a sudden stop.

Zak scratched his head. 'There's something wrong with the computer!'

'No, I don't think that's the problem,' Dr Trifle said, untying the rope from the pier. 'Okay, off you go. Goodbye! And please be careful with Selby. He doesn't know how to swim.'

'That's all right, Dr T,' Zak called back. 'We can't swim either.'

The *Sleek Geek* sailed out of the harbour and into the open sea. The DogsBody people played with their laptops as they passed one yacht after another.

'This is soooooooo good,' Selby thought as he lay on the deck, his ears flapping in the gentle breeze while he watched the sunlight dancing on the waves. 'My brain just went on holiday. Come to think of it, so did this dog's body.'

Later on, Selby and the others went down into the cabin.

'Time for lunch,' Miles said, opening some

packets and tipping them into bowls. 'Uh–oh, I think we forgot to buy dog food.'

'I guess Selby will just have to eat people food,' Eva said. 'Hey, look, you guys! Selby just ate a couple of pretzels and now he's eating chips! He seems to like our food. We'll microwave the pizza later.'

'Oh joy, oh joy,' Selby thought. 'These computer dudes may not know anything about sailing but they sure do know how to eat.'

And on they ate till empty packets and cold pizza slices covered the little table.

'Hey, guys,' Eva said, pushing some buttons on the little computer. 'At this rate, TINY says we'll win easily. Five days, three hours, fifteen minutes and three seconds — it'll be a record.'

A helicopter from a television station buzzed overhead taking pictures for the evening news and then sped off.

Selby went back on deck to soak up the last rays of the afternoon sun. There was no land in sight now, just waves, waves and more waves.

'This is the life,' he thought. 'I wish this could go on for months, or even years.'

For the next two days the *Sleek Geek* sliced its way onward as the last of the seagulls turned back towards land. The DogsBody people cuddled Selby and patted him while playing their computer games and feeding him more chips, more dips and many many slices of pizza.

'I don't think I can handle another chip or slice of pizza,' Selby thought. 'How can these guys eat this stuff all day every day? How can they drink all those fizzy drinks? Right now I'd eat a plateful of brussel sprouts. Even a Dry-Mouth Dog Biscuit would look good.'

That afternoon the waves got bigger and the yacht pitched and rolled. One by one, the DogsBody people took off their headphones and looked up from their laptops.

'Gosh!' Miles said. 'We sure are tipping a long way over.'

'We sure are,' Zak agreed. 'You don't think we could tip right over, do you?'

Once again, Eva touched the little screen on TINY the computer.

'Don't worry. If we lean over any more then TINY will pull in some of those pieces of cloth and we'll go back up straight again.'

'But what if a big wave comes along and slams into us from the side and we tip upside-down?' Miles asked.

Eva pulled out her pocket calculator and punched the keys.

'The chance of a big wave coming along is only one in seven hundred and sixty-two,' she said. 'And I'm sure TINY would know what to do to keep us from going over.'

'Gulp,' Selby gulped. 'One chance in seven hundred and sixty-two. Why couldn't she just have said it's impossible?'

That night, as the others slept in their bunks, Selby lay wide awake feeling the boat roll from side to side.

'I just hope TINY knows what it's doing,' he thought. 'If only I could just forget about it and get some sleep. All that horrible junk food is upsetting my tummy. And all this rolling from side to side is making it worse. What I need is a nice cup of warm milk. Warm milk always helps me get to sleep.'

It was while Selby was reaching up to get the milk out of the fridge that it happened. Suddenly, the one-in-seven-hundred-and-sixty-two-of-a-chance wave slammed into the side of the *Sleek Geek*. TINY quickly blinked into action, turning the boat sharply. And that would have been okay except the sudden movement made Selby drop the carton of milk. And that still would have been okay if the milk hadn't spilled all over TINY.

Motors whirred, booms boomed and the rudder rudded violently.

'Oh, no!' Selby thought. 'The computer's gone bonkers!'

Miles sat up in his bunk.

'What's happening?' he said.

'Something's wrong with TINY,' Eva answered.

There was a loud *crunch*! and then another *crunch*! as water spurted up through the floor of the cabin.

'We've hit something! Everybody out!' Miles cried.

Selby scrambled up onto the deck with the DogsBody people close behind. The boat bashed against the rocks of an island. Selby clung in panic to a rope and watched as pieces of the yacht were torn away.

'The *Sleek Geek* is breaking up!' he screamed in his brain. 'I've got to get off this death trap!'

'Jump to the rocks!' Eva shouted. 'Everyone jump!'

The *Sleek* Geek heaved forward and the DogsBody people jumped onto the rocks. Selby hesitated as the yacht was dragged away again. Another wave crashed into the side of the boat, slamming it against the rocks and knocking Selby over. He struggled to his feet as two waves swept over the *Sleek Geek*, pulling it further from shore.

'Oh, no!' Selby thought. 'I left it too late!'

'Come on, Selby!' Zak yelled. 'Jump!'

'I can't!' Selby thought. 'It's too far to jump now!'

Suddenly a huge wave roared in, crashing down on what was left of the yacht.

It was a terrified dog that leapt for his life, shooting through the air like a lost cannonball, and landing right in the arms of Eva.

'Gotcha!' she said. 'Hey, good jump, Sel! That was neat!'

As the sun rose the next morning, the DogsBody people sat shivering on the beach, brushing the sand from their wet clothes. Selby followed as they got up and wandered silently around the little island.

Jason was the first to speak.

'Far out,' he said.

Zak spoke next.

'Amazing,' he said.

Then it was Miles' turn.

'What are the odds of this happening?' he asked.

Eva's pocket calculator had survived the shipwreck.

'Nine hundred thousand to one,' she said.

'Forget the odds,' Selby thought. 'It's happened.'

Selby looked at the DogsBody people who by this time were sitting quietly with their heads in their hands.

'They have no idea what to do,' he thought. 'But who am I to talk? I don't either. And it's all my fault. I should never have got the milk out of the fridge. Who said you shouldn't cry over spilt milk? (*Sniff*) Watch me.'

Now, if you or I were stranded on a tiny, out-of-the-way island, we'd look for fresh water to drink and fruits to eat or we'd try to catch fish.

'These guys wouldn't recognise food unless it came in a packet,' Selby sighed.

And, if you or I were stranded and there was nothing to eat or drink, we'd at least play games or sing songs to cheer ourselves up and hope that we'd be rescued.

'These guys wouldn't recognise a game unless it had a joystick and a keyboard,' Selby thought. 'And they've been listening to their music players for so long they've never learned how to sing.'

A day passed but no one came to find them. Their clothes — and Selby's fur — dried in the warm breeze but still they just sat and stared at the sea. Selby slept badly that night. Tears filled his eyes as he thought about his cozy home in Bogusville and the wonderful Trifles.

In the morning, he sat wondering how he'd got himself into this mess.

'I never should have sent my photo to DogsBody,' he thought. 'These guys didn't need a symbol. What they needed was a nanny. I mean, they're really smart but they still need someone to tell them what to do.'

Just as he was thinking this thought, Selby heard a faint buzzing sound in the distance.

'What do you reckon that is?' Eva asked.

'It sounds like a helicopter,' Jason said.

'It *is* a helicopter!' Selby thought as he saw a speck coming closer and closer. 'It's coming to get us!'

The helicopter was about to pass over them.

'They'll never see us,' Zak said with a sigh. 'They're up too high.'

'Come on, guys!' Selby thought. 'Don't just sit there like a bunch of lumps! Wave your arms! Run around! Do something!'

Selby ran out onto the beach.

'What's Selby doing?' Eva asked.

'I don't know,' Zak said. 'He's kinda running but he's digging at the same time. It's like he's gone crazy or something.'

'Far out,' Jason said.

'Hea-*vy*,' Miles added.

The DogsBody people sat there stunned as Selby tore around and around the sand making a sound that sounded something like *eeeeeeeeeeeeeaaaaaaaaauuuuuuuuuuuuwwwwwwwww*!

Round and round he went, turning this way

and that, digging a trench in the sand as he went.

Then, just as the helicopter was turning to leave, it suddenly spun around and started down.

'It's seen us!' Zak yelled. 'It's coming to rescue us!'

Soon the helicopter had landed on the beach. The cheering DogsBody people picked up Selby and scrambled inside.

'Thank goodness you saw us,' Eva said to the pilot as the helicopter zoomed up into the sky again.

'I didn't see you,' the pilot said. 'I saw your dog's body.'

'You saw him?' Zak asked, pointing to Selby.

'No,' the pilot said, 'I couldn't have seen him from up where I was. He's too small. I saw your dog's body. The picture on the beach. That thing you had on your sail.' He pointed towards the ground. 'As soon as I saw it, I knew you must be on the island.'

The DogsBody people (and Selby) looked down at the beach. There, below, was an outline in the sand looking very much like Selby.

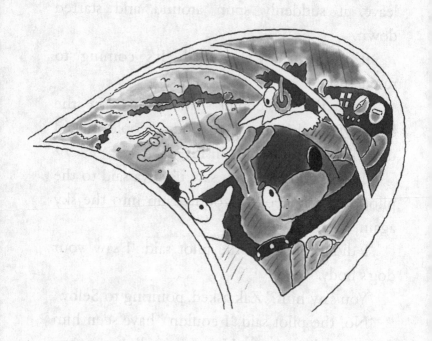

'Wow!' Miles said. 'We didn't do that! Selby
must have done it when he ran around and
around in the sand.'

'And it came out looking just like him,' Zak
said.

'Yes,' Eva said, getting out her calculator. 'What do you reckon the chances of that would be?'

'That's something you'll never know,' Selby thought.

And now he felt a warm feeling come over him. He was going home.

GARY GAGGS AND THE GHOSTLY GAGSTER

'My last comedy show was a disaster!' cried Gary Gaggs. 'I'm going to give up being a comedian.'

Dr and Mrs Trifle both smiled while Selby struggled not to smile.

'I just love this guy,' Selby thought. 'He can make anything funny. I can't wait for the punchline.'

'Well?' Mrs Trifle said. 'What's the punchline?'

'There is no punchline,' Gary said. 'I'm serious. Every time I do my show, it's a total disaster.'

'You haven't been telling your killer joke 🐾 again, have you?' Mrs Trifle asked.

'No, someone is coming to all my shows and shouting out my punchlines before I can say them.'

'Oh, so it's a heckler,' Mrs Trifle said. 'But you've got all those great put-down lines to make hecklers feel silly.'

'Yes,' Dr Trifle agreed. 'Remember the heckler with the big nose and you said, *Excuse me, sir, but is that your nose or are you eating a banana?* And another time when there was a heckler with big ears and you said, *Are those your ears or is there an elephant standing behind you?* That was very funny.'

'I remember a heckler who was wearing a shirt with wide stripes,' Mrs Trifle said. 'He started yelling things out and you said, *Excuse me, sir, but is that a striped shirt or am I looking through the bars of your cage?*'

'I've got lots of heckler busters 🐾 🐾,' Gary said, 'but they're no good because I can't see

🐾 *Paw note: See the story 'Selby's Shemozzle' in the book Selby's Shemozzle.*

🐾 🐾 *There are more of Gary's heckler busters at the end of this book.*

S

21

who's heckling. It's like he's a phantom heckler. He's a ghostly gagster. He knows all my jokes and he's following me around.'

'Sheeesh!' Selby thought, as a shiver shot up his spine. 'A phantom heckler. A ghostly gagster. That gives me the creeps.'

'It happened in Brisbane and then in Sydney just last week,' Gary said. 'Someone must really hate me.'

'That's silly,' Mrs Trifle said. 'Everybody loves a comedian.'

'Everyone except *another* comedian,' Gary said.

'I reckon he's right,' Selby thought. 'I'll bet it's a jealous comedian turning up to his shows and ruining them.'

'You could make up new jokes for every show,' Dr Trifle suggested. 'That way he wouldn't know the punchlines.'

'That would be impossible. Do you know how long it takes to make up a whole show full of jokes?' Gary sighed. 'Will you guys do me a favour? Would you come to my show this afternoon and see if you can spot the heckler and point him out to me? It's hard for me to see because of the spotlights on stage shining in my eyes.'

'You can count on us, Gary,' Mrs Trifle said. 'We'll be there.'

'And so will I,' thought Selby. 'But I'll have to sneak in.'

That afternoon, Dr and Mrs Trifle and Gary drove to the theatre together. Selby ran after them, taking every short-cut that he could think of.

'I've never been this nervous in my life,' Gary admitted.

'Relax,' Mrs Trifle said. 'We'll find your phantom heckler for you and then you can give him your best heckler busters.'

Selby crept into the theatre and hid behind the curtain so that he could peek out at everyone in the audience.

'Good afternoon, ladies and germs,' Gary said starting the show. 'It's great to be back in Bogusville. This is where I did my very first comedy show. You may not know this but I wasn't always a comedian. No, I wasn't. I used to be a tailor but I had to quit. It didn't suit me. It

23

didn't *suit* me. Woo woo woo!' Gary added, strutting around like a chicken.

'Oh! Oh! Oh!' Selby gasped. 'It didn't *suit* him. That's great!'

'But seriously, folks, then I got a job in a bag factory but they gave me the sack.'

'The bag factory gave him the *sack*!' Selby thought, as he struggled not to laugh.

'Then I worked in a fruit-juice factory but they *canned* me. I just couldn't *concentrate*. Woo woo woo!'

'Gary has to be the funniest guy in the whole world!' Selby thought, as the audience roared with laughter. 'And they're loving it!'

Selby looked all around the audience. Everyone was laughing except one silver-haired old man with a pimple on his nose.

'He isn't even smiling,' Selby thought. 'He might be a bit deaf, poor guy.'

'But seriously, folks,' Gary went on. 'Two fish were in a tank. One of the fish said to the other fish, "How do you drive this thing?" Woo woo woo!'

'I get it!' Selby thought. 'They were in a *tank*! An army tank! That is soooooooo funny! And

24

Gary was worried for nothing. The heckler isn't even here today.'

'I have this hopeless little brother named Larry,' Gary continued. 'One day I saw him carrying a ladder to school. A big, tall ladder. So I said, "Where are you going with that?" And Larry said —'

Suddenly a voice from the audience yelled out, 'I need it because I'm starting *high* school today!'

'It's him!' Selby thought. 'It's the phantom heckler! He's here, after all!'

The audience laughed as they looked around.

'But seriously, folks,' Gary said, ignoring the heckler. 'My brother was taking an exam and the teacher said to him, "I hope I didn't just see you copying Melanie's answers." And Larry said —'

'*I hope you didn't either*!' the heckler shouted.

'Yes, very good,' Gary said. 'You took the words right out of my mouth. Anyway, that evening Mum asked him if the exam questions were hard. And he said, "No, the questions were simple —"'

'*It's just the answers that were hard*!' the voice yelled out.

'I couldn't have put it better myself,' Gary said, pretending to laugh along with the audience.

'I can't believe this,' Selby thought. 'He's telling the punchlines to every one of Gary's jokes. I can't see who's doing it and neither can anyone else.'

'But seriously, folks,' Gary went on. 'One day my brother rang the principal. He put on a deep voice and said, "Larry is sick today so he can't go to school." So the principal said, "Okay, but who is this calling?" And my brother said — '

Once again the phantom heckler yelled out. '*It's my father!*'

'Poor Gary,' Selby thought. 'He's so stressed.'

After the show, the Trifles met Gary in his dressing room.

'Sorry, Gary,' Mrs Trifle said. 'We couldn't figure out where the voice was coming from.'

'Well, he got what he wanted,' said Gary. 'Because I quit. I'm never going to do another comedy show.'

'Gary, that's terrible! And what about tonight's show? You can't just not turn up. It's sold out. Some people will have driven for hours to see you.'

'Then they can have their money back,' Gary said.

'Gary, please,' Mrs Trifle said. 'Whoever he is, he won't come back again tonight, I'm sure.'

'I'm sure he will.'

'How long have we known each other?'

'I don't know. Almost all our lives. Why?'

'Then do us a big friends' favour,' Mrs Trifle said. 'Do your show this one last time and we'll find the heckler — we promise.'

Selby was on his way home from the show when it happened. He was passing the old man he'd seen in the theatre, the old man who hadn't laughed at Gary's jokes. Only now he was laughing.

'*Ha ha ha ha*. That was so funny!' the man said out loud. 'It was all I could do to keep from laughing.'

'What is it with this guy?' Selby thought. 'He doesn't even smile through the whole show and now he's laughing like a kookaburra.'

'The more I think about those jokes, the funnier they get,' the man said. '*Ha ha ha ha*.'

Selby looked back over his shoulder at the man.

'Hey, this guy's talking and laughing and everything — without moving his lips. Like a ventriloquist.'

Selby stopped dead in his tracks.

'That's it!' he thought. 'He *is* a ventriloquist! He's the ghostly gagster! I've got to do something about this!'

'Hello there, old boy,' the man said to Selby. 'What are you looking at? Come here. I want to give you a pat.'

'Whoa! He can't be a ventriloquist,' Selby thought. 'His lips didn't even twitch when he said *boy* and *pat*. Even a ventriloquist can't do that. I've got to find out more about this dude.'

Selby ducked into the bushes and followed the man to the Bogusville Motel. He stood on his hind legs and peered into the man's window.

Moments later, he watched in shock as the old man stood in front of his mirror and grabbed his face, pulling it off along with his gray hair. Underneath was a younger man.

'It's a mask!' Selby gasped. 'No wonder he

could talk without moving his lips! Selby, the dog detective 🐾, strikes again!'

That evening, Gary found a mysterious note in his dressing room. It read:

The heckler weare a mask. Look
for an old man with silver hair and a pimple
on his nose.

'So that's how he does it!' Gary cried. 'But I wonder who wrote this note.'

'Not us,' said the Trifles.

'Well, whoever did,' Gary said, 'just saved my career. If this masked man turns up at my show tonight, I'll be ready for him.'

Once again, Dr and Mrs Trifle were in the theatre, watching the audience. And, once again, Selby watched from behind the curtain.

'Every seat is filled and I still don't see the gagster,' Selby thought. 'That's strange. Maybe he's not coming, after all.'

Finally, Gary came out onto the stage.

🐾 *Paw note: See the story 'Selby Supersnoop, Dog Detective' in the book* Selby Supersnoop.

S

29

'Good evening, ladies and jellyfish,' he said. 'It's great to be back in Bogusville. This is where I did my very first comedy show. You may not know this but I wasn't always a comedian. I used to work at a garage installing mufflers but it was exhausting. It was *exhausting*! Woo woo woo!'

'I haven't heard that one before,' Selby thought. 'He's got so many great jokes.'

'But seriously, folks,' Gary went on. 'I wanted to be a musician but my piano playing wasn't *note*worthy. Woo woo woo! So I went to work in a shoe factory but I didn't *fit* in. Then I tried to be a witch. I only did that for a *spell*. For a while I worked at the zoo feeding the giraffes but I just wasn't *up* to it. Woo woo woo! I thought you'd like that one.'

'*Like* it?' Selby screamed in his brain. 'I *loved* it.'

'But seriously, folks. I tried to be a doctor but I just didn't have the *patients*. And then I was a history teacher for a while but I didn't think there was any *future* in it.'

'Gary has to be the funniest funnyman in the whole world,' Selby thought as he bit his tongue to keep from laughing out loud. 'I can barely stand it!'

After a while, Gary said, 'My hopeless little brother, Larry, had his first day at school. Mum asked him, "Was it fun?" And my brother said —'

Before Gary could say another word, a voice from the audience yelled out, '*Yes, but someone called Miss kept spoiling it.*'

'It's him again!' Selby thought.

'Thank you,' Gary said with a laugh. 'My little brother was so dumb that he thought that a traffic jam was —'

'*Something police officers put on their toast!*' the voice yelled out.

Selby's eyes darted from one person to the next.

'I can't see who's doing it,' he thought.

Gary went on. 'My hopeless little brother thought that a see-saw was —'

'*Something you cut water with!*' the heckler yelled.

'No wonder I didn't see him!' Selby thought. 'He's dressed like a woman this time! He's about three rows back. No one's spotted him! I've got to stop him before he ruins Gary's act again.'

Selby slipped silently along the row just behind the ghostly gagster.

'This is him, I know it is!' Selby looked up at the woman's hair hanging down over the back of the seat. 'I'll just wait a second to be sure.'

'One day Larry and I were getting dressed to go to school,' Gary said, 'and I said, "Hey, you've got holes in your underwear." And he said —'

'Here I go!' Selby thought. 'Selby to the rescue!'

And the voice yelled out, '*Of course I've got holes in my underwear. How do you think I —*'

As soon as those words were out of his mouth, the man felt a sudden tug from behind that pulled off his wig and his mask at the same time.

'How do you think I get my feet into them . . .' the man said, his voice getting slower and lower as he went. 'Hey! What's going on here?!'

As Selby crept quietly beneath the seats, the man suddenly stood up. Gary Gaggs stared at him in disbelief.

'Larry!' he cried. 'It's you, my own brother! You're the one who's been ruining my shows! Why? Why did you do it?'

Larry's face turned pink, then red and then deep purple. Tears formed in his eyes.

'Because you're not nice,' he sobbed. 'Just because you're Mr Big Famous Comedian doesn't mean you can be cruel to your little brother.'

'Oh, Larry,' Gary said, stepping off the stage. 'I was just joking.'

'Jokes can hurt people, you know.'

'I'm so sorry,' Gary said, giving his brother a big hug. 'I had no idea I was hurting your feelings. I promise I'll never tell jokes about you again. Will you forgive me?'

'Yes,' Larry said, blowing his nose, 'if you'll forgive me for ruining your shows.'

And, as Selby slipped secretly out from beneath the seats, he heard the loudest clapping and cheering that he'd ever heard at one of Gary's comedy shows.

'Isn't that lovely?' Selby thought as he too felt tears come to his eyes. 'I think this was Gary's greatest show ever.'

THE SEARCH FOR SELBY

'This is seriously weird!' Selby gasped. 'Suddenly there are dogs all over town — huge dogs! They're everywhere! We're in the middle of a dog invasion!'

Two dogs stopped in the street.

'*Arf!*' one of them said. 'I'm Figaro.'

'*Bow wow*,' the other one answered. 'I'm Piddles. Pleased to meet you. Have you seen Kewpie?'

'Is she the Irish Setter?'

'No, she's the Wolfhound Pomeranian cross.'

'I think she's at the Convention Centre.'

'What is happening here?!' Selby screamed in his brain. 'They're not only dogs — they're *talking* dogs, just like me! I thought I was the only talking dog in Australia and, perhaps, the world!'

Selby stood there, stunned, as dogs passed him on the footpath.

'Wait just a minute,' he thought. 'There's something wrong here. They're all walking on their hind legs. Maybe they're walking on their *only* legs. I reckon they're people in dog suits and not dogs at all. Phew! I'm glad I didn't talk to them because I'd have given away my secret.'

'It's the annual meeting of the SSS,' Mrs Trifle explained to Dr Trifle later that day. 'They're the first group to hire the new Convention Centre.'

'I didn't expect the Centre to be hired by people in dog suits,' Dr Trifle said. 'I thought it would be for people selling tractors or for sheep-shearing demonstrations. What exactly does SSS stand for, anyway?'

'It's the Search for Selby Society.'

'Gulp,' Selby gulped.

'Who is this Selby 🐾?' Dr Trifle asked.

🐾 *Paw note: Of course the Trifles only know my real name — which isn't Selby. They don't know that I ring up Duncan and tell him my stories so that he can write these books. Duncan knows that my name's not really Selby, but even he doesn't know what it really is.* S

'You know, the dog in those children's books. The SSS is looking for him.'

'Double gulp,' Selby gulped again. 'They're after me!'

'But Selby is just a made-up character,' Dr Trifle said. 'Surely they don't think he's real.'

'Yes, they do. These people used to be in a group that searched for alien life forms in other parts of the universe, but they gave up.'

'Why did they give up?'

'Because they didn't find any. Then one of them said, "Why are we looking for alien life forms off in space when there might be some right here on earth?"'

'Good point . . . I guess,' Dr Trifle said.

'Then someone read one of the Selby books and thought that maybe they're true. Maybe an alien has taken over a dog's body right here in Australia and that Selby is him.'

'Now, hold the show!' Selby thought. 'I'm not an alien life form. I'm a normal dog who just happens to know how to talk.'

'But why do they wear dog suits?' Dr Trifle asked. 'They certainly seem like a bunch of odd bods.'

'No, I think they're quite normal people but they might be embarrassed to let their friends know about their hobby of looking for aliens. Some of them might actually be famous people. Anyway, when they go to meetings, they put on dog suits and use made-up dog names.'

'Why did they choose Bogusville ✤ for their meeting?'

'Apparently Bogusville is a lot like the town in the Selby books,' Mrs Trifle explained. 'And, by the way, I've invited some of them around for afternoon tea.'

'They're coming here?'

'Just a few of them,' Mrs Trifle said. 'When I told them we have a dog, they seemed very excited to meet him.'

'I'll bet they were,' Selby silently moaned.

'How old is he?' Candy asked when the group from SSS arrived.

> ✤ *Paw note: The town I live in isn't really called Bogusville. I made that up when I started telling my stories to Duncan so that he wouldn't be able to find me.* S

'He's ten,' Mrs Trifle said, passing around a plate of biscuits.

'Why, that's the same age as Selby in the books!'

Bambino struggled to drink her tea through the mouth of her dog suit and then said, 'He's a very clean dog.'

'Have you ever wondered,' BeoWoof asked, 'if he might be inhabited by an alien?'

'Oh, puleeeez,' Selby thought.

'No, not really,' Dr Trifle said, 'but strange things sometimes happen when Selby's around.'

BeoWoof, Sausage, Tofu, Candy, Bambino and Fang put down their teacups.

'What sort of strange things?' asked Fang.

'Yes, what sort of strange things?' Selby thought.

'Oh, just little things, like the times we've come home and found the lights and TV on when we thought we'd turned them off.'

'You call those *little* things?' asked Tofu.

'Well, yes,' Mrs Trifle answered, 'because we know that we must have left them on. It obviously can't have been Selby who turned them on while we were out.'

'I'm not so sure about that,' Bambino said. 'When the TV was on, was Selby anywhere near it?'

'Yes, but then he does spend a lot of time in the loungeroom, don't you, Selby?'

'Why did you ask him a question?' Candy asked. 'Do you expect him to answer you?'

'Of course not,' Mrs Trifle laughed. 'We often ask him questions. He never answers. It's just a silly thing we do.'

'It might not be that silly,' Sausage said. 'We think that people sense when their pets are inhabited by alien life forms.'

'I'm not an alien life form!' Selby thought. 'When are these people going to leave me alone?'

'Could you explain that?' asked Mrs Trifle.

'People are very sensitive,' Sausage said. 'We sense when aliens are near. I think you must sense that Selby can understand everything you say and that's why you talk to him.'

There was a long silence as the Search for Selby Society dog-people stared at Selby.

'Stop doing that!' Selby thought. 'You're going to make me blush!'

'Well then,' Mrs Trifle said, changing the subject. 'What happens at your meetings?'

'Mostly we talk about the clues in the Selby books,' BeoWoof said.

'Yes,' Candy agreed. 'We study the books to see if there are any clues as to what Selby's real name might be and where he lives and who his owners are. The author of the books says that Selby's a real dog and that he knows how to talk, and we have no reason to doubt that.'

'And sooner or later he will give himself away and we'll find him,' Fang added. 'Isn't that right, Selby?'

'Oh, no!' Selby screamed in his brain. 'I wish they'd stop staring at me and go to their silly meeting. Come to think of it, I'm the one who should go to their meeting. I should go and see if they're about to spring me. But how can I be there without being noticed?'

It was a secretive dog that crept under the house and quietly put on the dog-suit disguise that he kept hidden there. And it was a nervous dog-suited dog that walked into the Convention Centre.

Selby sat and listened to one speaker after another talking about the clues they'd found in the Selby books.

'I had no idea I gave away that much!' Selby thought. 'I'm going to have to stop telling Duncan my stories. These people have almost enough clues to find me! This is awful. (*Sniff*) I'll have to leave home and never come back.'

Selby felt the tears running down his cheeks inside his dog suit at the thought of never seeing the Trifles again.

'Well, that ends our meeting for this year,' a man named Bazooka said. 'Bit by bit we've found out where he *can't* be. One good clue and we could find exactly where he is. We'll see you all next year. Keep in touch by email.'

'Excuse me,' Tofu said, 'but haven't we forgotten to look in the most obvious place of all?'

'What do you mean?'

'We chose to have our meeting in Bogusville because it's one of the nineteen towns around Australia that could be Selby's home. What if he actually does live here?'

'Yes, we know that's possible.'

'Well, if you were Selby and we came to your town, where would you be?'

'I'm not sure.'

'You'd come to the meeting, wouldn't you? You'd want to see what was going on. And we know from the Selby books that the first thing he'd do is to put on his dog suit so that people would think that he's a person in a dog suit. They wouldn't suspect that he's a *dog* in a dog suit 🐾.'

'You mean that he could be here right now?'

An excited murmur passed through the audience.

'Yes,' Tofu said. 'In fact, he could be you! Or you! Or you!' he said, pointing around the room, and finally pointing to Selby. 'Or you!' he added.

'Yeah, well he could be you, too!' Selby said, pointing back at him.

'He's right!' someone yelled. 'Let's take off our dog suits and see if there's a dog in here.'

'Take your own off,' someone else yelled back. 'You're not touching mine!'

🐾 *Paw note: For another story about me wearing my dog suit, see 'Tricks and Treats' in the book* Selby Snaps!

S

'Oh, so you're him!' another person yelled. 'Grab him and take off his head!'

'Oh no you don't!'

Soon there were people crash-tackling other people and pulling off their dog heads.

'Kirsty Karpenter!' a man's voice said. 'You're on that TV show about home renovations.'

'And who are you?' Kirsty said, grabbing the man's dog head and pulling it off. 'Hey! Aren't you the weatherman on Channel 8?'

'Don't you dare tell anyone that I'm here!' the man said.

One by one, heads were removed until finally they were down to the last dog suit. A dog suit that was running for the door.

'Hey! Stop that dog!' someone yelled. 'Stop him, Fang!'

'Oh no you don't!' a voice yelled back. 'You're not taking my head off!'

'It must be him! It must be the real Selby!'

The little figure started running faster, punching and kicking its way through the crowd, knocking people this way and that.

'We've finally got him! Don't let him get away!'

'If I can only get through that door,' he muttered, 'they'll never catch me. Out of my way!'

But it was no use. There was only one of him and now the whole dog-headless Search for Selby Society pounced, knocking him to the floor. Within a second, someone had ripped off his dog-head.

There was a huge gasp.

'It's–it's *him*!' someone stammered, 'It's the *Prime Minister*! We had no idea you were in the Search for Selby Society!'

'Well, now you do,' he said, dusting himself off. 'Now will someone give me my head back? My limousine is waiting.'

'Apparently it was a very exciting meeting,' Mrs Trifle said to Dr Trifle after the Search for Selby Society had left town. 'There's a rumour that even the Prime Minister is in the group and he was there. I think he may even have been one of the people who came here for afternoon tea.'

'Goodness me!' Dr Trifle said. 'Who would have expected it?'

'Certainly not me,' Mrs Trifle said. 'And they were a very neat and tidy group. They didn't leave any rubbish behind at the Convention Centre. The only thing that was left behind was a dog suit. Someone found it by the back window. I put it in the Lost and Found but nobody's come to claim it.'

'And I don't think that anyone will,' Selby thought, as he lay on the carpet remembering his narrow escape when he slipped out of the dog suit and jumped out the window of the Convention Centre. 'But at least I know exactly where the dog suit is for the next time I need it.'

SELBY SHORN

'How can you possibly help Shawn the shearer?' Mrs Trifle asked. 'You've never shorn a sheep in your life.'

It was a beautiful sunny day and the Trifles were driving out to the country. Selby lay on the back seat half asleep.

'No, I haven't,' Dr Trifle admitted. 'Shawn will do the shearing. But remember, I'm an inventor and I've brought along my newly-invented EPFD to help him.'

'EPFD? What does that stand for? Knowing the way you name your inventions, it's probably an Ever Popular Fur Demolisher or something like that.'

'That's close,' Dr Trifle admitted. 'It stands for

Easy Peasy Fleece Decreaser. The idea is to help Shawn set a sheep-shearing record.'

'A shearing record? But won't it be cheating to use a machine? Isn't that like using roller skates to win a running race?'

'No, no. First of all my EPFD isn't really a machine. It's just sort of a *device*.'

'I don't understand.'

'Here it is,' Dr Trifle said, taking a tiny black box out of his pocket. 'This will never even touch the sheep — or the shearer.'

'Then how does it work?'

Dr Trifle pressed a button on the box and suddenly there was a terrible scraping sound that sounded something like *skuuuurrrrreeeexxx!*

'Stop that!' Mrs Trifle screamed. 'I can't stand it!'

Selby suddenly sat up straight.

'Sheeesh! That was awful!' he thought. 'It sounded like fingernails scratching a blackboard.'

'That was terrible!' Mrs Trifle said. 'It sounded like fingernails scratching a blackboard.'

'You guessed it,' Dr Trifle said. 'That's exactly what it is. This EPFD is just a mini-recorder.

I recorded the sound of my fingernails scratching a blackboard.'

'Well, it's a horrible sound!' Mrs Trifle said. 'It made the hairs on my arms stand up. And look at poor Selby,' she said, looking in the rear-vision mirror. 'All his fur is standing on end.'

'That's the idea,' Dr Trifle said proudly. 'When each sheep is about to be shorn, I'll push the button and the sheep's fleece will stand up straight. This will make it very easy for Shawn to shear it.'

'How about poor Shawn? If he has to listen to that all day long, he'll go bonkers.'

'I've thought of that. I've brought along earplugs for everyone — but not for the sheep, of course.'

'And probably not for me, either,' Selby thought.

Soon they turned up the long driveway into the Me & Ewes Sheep Station. Selby watched as the sheep dogs herded a flock of sheep towards the shearing shed.

'Look at all those sheep!' Selby thought. 'I wonder if they know they're all about to have a haircut.'

'G'day,' Shawn called out. 'Great to see you, Doc. Did you bring the thingy?'

'Yes, I did,' said Dr Trifle. 'Show me to the sheep and let's get shearing.'

Selby followed Shawn and the Trifles into the shed and watched them all put in their earplugs. Dr Trifle then pushed the button on his Easy Peasy Fleece Decreaser.

Skuuuurrrrreeeexxx!

'Oh, that's painful!' Selby thought, covering his ears with his paws.

'Start the clock!' Shawn yelled, grabbing his clippers. 'And bring on the sheep!'

Shawn grabbed the first sheep and flipped it on its back. Dr Trifle pushed the button.

Skuuuurrrrreeeexxx!

The sheep's wool sprang up straight. Shawn turned on his clippers with a *click* and a *hummmmmmmmm* and ran them quickly back and forth till the fleece fell neatly on the floor.

'This is great!' Shawn screamed, pushing the sheep down a chute and grabbing another. 'If I can keep this up, I reckon I'll beat the record!'

Skuuuurrrrreeeexxx!

Hummmmmmmmm.

51

'I'd love to stay and watch but I can't stand the noise,' Selby thought as he trotted outside. 'I'll watch the action out here instead.'

And action there was. Selby watched the sheep being herded into the shed and then shooting out again after they had been shorn.

'Poor little critters,' he thought. 'They look all bald and miserable now. I hope they're not too cold tonight. I'm just glad they don't shear dogs.'

As the day went on, Selby lay in the dirt watching the dogs work and listening to the screech of the EPFD.

'How am I doing?' Shawn yelled.

'Thirty-three seconds for that one!' Dr Trifle yelled back. 'Keep this up and you'll break the record of nine hundred and ninety-nine sheep in eight hours!'

'Wow!' Shawn screamed. 'And it's all thanks to you, Dr T! Shove another sheep over here!'

Skuuuurrrrreeeexxx!

Hummmmmmmmm.

And so it continued through the afternoon.

Skuuuurrrrreeeexxx!

Hummmmmmmmm.

Skuuuurrrrreeeexxx!

Hummmmmmmmm.

Skuuuurrrrreeeexxx!

Hummmmmmmmm.

Selby covered his ears with his paws and peeked into the shed.

'Watch him go!' Selby thought. 'I can barely see him because of the wool in the air. It's like a blizzard in there!'

'Ten more minutes!' Dr Trifle yelled. 'Shear sixteen more and you'll break the world record! You're going to do it!'

'Hey, only sixteen more,' Selby thought. 'Oops, we have a problem. There's only ten left. He's going to run out of sheep! This is a tragedy! It's a catastrophe!'

Selby looked all around the paddock. Suddenly he noticed something moving up on the hillside.

'There are more sheep up there,' he thought. 'The dogs don't see them.'

'Come on, guys!' he called out to the dogs. 'Forget about these ones! Look! Up there! Go get 'em! This is hopeless. They're not even listening to me. Oh well. Here goes nothing . . .'

With this, Selby tore across the paddock and up the hill to where the sheep stood in the shade of the bushes.

'Okay, you lot,' he said. 'Time to get moving!'

Selby barked a couple of barks but the sheep just looked at him.

'Come on. I'm doing you a favour. You'll feel much better with those winter coats off. *Woof! Woof! Woof!*'

The sheep looked startled but kept staring at him.

'No more Mister Nice Dog. Get moving or get nipped!'

Selby snapped at the back of the sheep's legs and started chasing them down the hill.

'That's more like it. Now head for the shed.'

Selby and his sheep were partway down the hillside when the other dogs joined in.

'Hey, this is fun,' Selby thought, as the other dogs and he ran back and forth, driving the sheep across the paddock and up to the shed door. 'I feel like I'm part of a team. I'm a real working dog!'

The last few sheep squeezed through the small door as Selby and the other dogs circled back and forth.

'Nine hundred and ninety-seven!' Mrs Trifle screamed. 'Two minutes to go! You're going to hit one thousand! You'll break the world record!'

'Come on, Shawn!' Dr Trifle yelled. 'Go go go!'

'Uh-oh and double uh-oh,' Selby thought. 'There are only two sheep left. We're a sheep short!'

As the last sheep disappeared into the shed, the dogs closed in on Selby, pushing him towards the door.

'Hey, stop it, guys! It's me! I'm not a sheep! I'm one of you! Stop nipping my legs! Get off me!'

Meanwhile, inside the shed, Shawn's clippers tore along the last sheep's stomach and sides.

'You're almost there,' Mrs Trifle yelled. 'Just one more sheep!'

Blinded by sweat and flying wool, Shawn the shearer grabbed what he thought was an odd-looking sheep and ran his clippers along it so fast that it couldn't think to blink. Dr and Mrs Trifle were coughing and spluttering now and squinting through a snowstorm of wool.

'Stop!' Selby yelled. 'I'm not a sheep! I'm Selby, the only talking dog in Australia and, perhaps, the world! Don't do this to me!'

But the sounds of Selby's cries were muffled by earplugs and lost in the *skuuuurrrrreeeexxx!* of Dr Trifle's invention and the *hummmmmmmmm* of Shawn's shears.

'Did you say something?' asked Mrs Trifle, as Shawn the shearer sent the shorn Selby sliding down the chute. 'Hey, that was a weird one.'

'It didn't look like a sheep at all,' Dr Trifle agreed. 'It looked more like a . . . a goat or something.'

'One thousand sheep in eight hours! I'm the champion!' Shawn screamed with joy. 'Thanks to you, Dr Trifle.'

And so it was that Selby found himself herded up a ramp by the sheep dogs and squeezed into the middle of a huge three-decker sheep truck. A very tired Shawn climbed into the cab.

'Where are you taking them?' Dr Trifle asked.

'A few kilometres from here,' Shawn the shearer said. 'Better grass over there.'

'Bring them to our place,' Dr Trifle said with a laugh. 'It'll save me cutting the lawn.'

As the truck pulled away, Selby heard the Trifles calling for him.

'Come on, Selby,' Mrs Trifle sang out. 'Time to go home now.'

'Where do you think he's got to?' Dr Trifle asked. 'It's not like him to wander off.'

'I'm here!' Selby yelled above the baa-ing. 'Let me out!'

Dr and Mrs Trifle stopped and looked around.

'Did you hear something?' Mrs Trifle asked.

'I can't hear you,' Dr Trifle said. 'Wait till this noisy truck has gone.'

'Look! There's that strange sheep in the truck. It looks like it's waving to us,' Mrs Trifle said. 'Selby, where are you? Come on, boy.'

'My owners didn't even recognise me,' Selby sniffed, as the truck drove away. 'This is awful. What am I going to do? I'm not a sheep. If I have to eat grass, I'll die. Oh woe woe woe . . .'

That would have been the end of the story and maybe even the end of Selby — but it wasn't. No, if it had been the end of Selby then he couldn't have rung me up and told me all about it. What happened next was stranger than what had happened before.

No sooner had Shawn the shearer stopped the truck than the day's work caught up with him.

'I can hardly keep my eyes open,' he mumbled. 'One thousand sheep. (Yawn.) Eight hours. (Yawn.) I'll just lie down on the seat and have a mini-sleep before I (yawn) put the sheep out —

It was a bald-looking dog that made his way into the cab of the truck and quietly turned the key in the ignition.

Back in Bogusville, Dr and Mrs Trifle were sleeping badly, worrying about Selby.

'We'll go back to Shawn's and look for him after breakfast,' Dr Trifle said the next morning. 'I hope he didn't try to find his own way home because he could be lost forever. That's strange. Do you hear something?'

Dr and Mrs Trifle opened the curtains to see Shawn's truck parked in the street and the house surrounded by sheep.

'We've been invaded by sheep!' Mrs Trifle cried. 'What's going on here?'

'I think I know,' Dr Trifle said. 'I think Shawn took me seriously when I said the grass needed cutting. This must be his way of thanking me for my help yesterday.'

'Yes, that's probably it,' Mrs Trifle agreed. 'And will you have a look at what's sleeping on Selby's mat. It's that strange-looking sheep . . .'

'Selby? Is that you?'

THE DAY MY BRAIN SLEPT IN

by Selby Trifle

This morning I got out of bed
And realised my brain was dead,
That I had somehow left behind
A major portion of my mind.

I stumbled when I tried to walk,
I couldn't eat, I couldn't talk,
So back I climbed into my bed
And let my brain rejoin my head.

SELBY TIES THE KNOT*

'Do you take this dog to be your wedded husband?'

'I do.'

Selby looked into her beautiful eyes as she slipped the ring onto his toe.

'I can't believe this is happening to me,' he thought. 'She is soooooooo wonderful! Oh, lucky lucky me.'

'And do you take this woman to be your wedded wife?' the man asked. 'Dr Trifle, would you please come up and answer for Selby?'

* Author note: Most of the stories that Selby tells me are short. But this one is long and I couldn't make it any shorter without ruining it. Sorry.

'If only I could say *I do* myself,' Selby thought. 'But I can't because then everyone would know my secret. They'd know that I'm not an ordinary non-talking, non-*I-do*-saying dog.'

Dr Trifle made his way to the front of the stage but Selby spoke first.

'*Woof*!' he said.

There was laughter all around as the man said, 'Never mind, Dr Trifle. I think Selby just answered for himself. I now pronounce you dog and wife.'

It had all started a week before when Mrs Trifle and Selby were watching a TV show called 'Mix 'n' Match Marriage'.

'How can you watch that rubbish?' Dr Trifle said. 'It's just about people getting married.'

'They're not just *any* people,' said Mrs Trifle. 'Last week they had the world's tallest woman marrying the world's shortest man. He wore stilts at the wedding so they could be the same height.'

'I hope they didn't get married just to be on TV.'

'No, I'm sure they were in love and were going to get married anyway. But the show paid for a big wedding and a honeymoon.'

'The next thing you know they'll have triplets marrying triplets,' Dr Trifle said.

'That happened two weeks ago. And three weeks ago a famous explorer married a camel driver. They dressed all the camels up as bridesmaids.'

'I don't know why you waste your time watching such a show.'

'Millions of people do,' Mrs Trifle said.

'And at least one dog,' thought Selby. 'I love watching weddings. They're fun. Everyone is always so happy that it makes me happy too.'

Selby looked at the smiling face of the presenter.

'And that's our show for today,' she said. 'Next week we'll be coming to you from the country town of Bogusville where we'll have the craziest wedding ever. This is Sibyl Sweetie. See you next week, and, if you have any wedding suggestions, send us a letter or an email.'

'Bogusville?' Dr Trifle said. 'Did you know the show was coming here?'

'As a matter of fact I did, because the producer phoned the Council about it.'

'So what's this crazy wedding all about?' Dr Trifle asked. 'We don't have any camel drivers or triplets here.'

'No, but we have dogs,' Mrs Trifle said.

'Dogs? What do you mean?'

'They're going to have the first-ever dog wedding on TV.'

'What dogs?'

'Hamish the sheepdog and Melanie Mildew's terrier, Posy,' Mrs Trifle said.

'Hamish and Posy?!' Dr Trifle exclaimed. 'But they can't get married. They're ... dogs!'

'It won't be a real marriage, of course,' Mrs Trifle said. 'Melanie and Hamish's owner will be paid some money and then they'll all go on a honeymoon cruise.'

'It sounds like just another silly thing to put on that very silly show so lots of silly people will watch it,' Dr Trifle said. 'Hamish and Posy. I wonder who came up with that idea.'

'Apparently a Mr S. Elby sent them a letter suggesting it and they liked it. Have you heard of a Mr S. Elby in Bogusville?'

'No, I don't think I have.'

Selby looked up innocently at the Trifles.

'Well I have,' he thought 🐾.

A week later, Bogusville Fairground was filled with television equipment and people organising the wedding. And, of course, everyone from Bogusville was there. Mrs Trifle had even talked Dr Trifle into coming and the Trifles and Selby were sitting in the front row of the stands.

'This is so much fun!' Selby thought. 'And it's all because of little old me. Oh, look, there's Sibyl! She looks even gorgeouser in real life than she does on TV.'

Hamish was on the stage with a hairdresser working furiously on his fur. Nearby, another hairdresser was putting a bow in Posy's fur.

'Quiet please, everyone!' Gus the producer said. 'We're on the air in five minutes. We'll do a quick run-through. Ms Mildew, could you please lead the bride dog up here?'

The orchestra started playing 'The Wedding

🐾 *Paw note: Remember that my real name isn't Selby so the Trifles wouldn't have known it was me.* S

March' while Melanie led Posy slowly down the aisle.

'Okay, so it's a bit silly,' Selby thought, 'but it still brings tears to my eyes.'

And that's when it happened . . .

No sooner did Posy sit next to Hamish than, without so much as a growl, she bit him. She bit him so hard that he yelped and tore off across the fairground.

'This is a disaster!' cried the producer. 'The show is ruined! I never should have listened to you, Sibyl. Dogs getting married is a silly idea!'

'You loved the idea,' Sibyl said. 'Stay cool. We just need another groom dog, that's all.'

The presenter looked around the audience.

'There's no time, Sibyl,' the producer said. 'We've got two minutes.'

'Him!' Sibyl said, suddenly pointing to Selby. 'Excuse me, sir. Would you mind if your dog got married?'

'Well, I don't know . . .' Dr Trifle began.

'*Yes! yes!* Say *yes!*' Selby thought.

'Yes, yes, of course!' Mrs Trifle said quickly. 'I'm sure Selby won't mind — as long as Posy doesn't bite him.'

'She won't bite me. I'll just give her my best *you'd-better-not-bite-me-or-else* look and she'll leave me alone. Hey, I'm going to be famous!' Selby thought as he struggled not to smile. 'This is fun!'

And it would have been fun, too, except that Selby's *you'd-better-not-bite-me-or-else* look worked too well. Instead of biting him, Posy panicked and started howling and pulling at her leash to get away.

'Okay, cancel the show,' the producer sighed. 'That's it. And you and I are out of a job, Sibyl.'

'No, no! I've got another idea.'

'I think I've had enough of your ideas.'

'This one is perfect — *I* will marry Selby.'

'You'll *whaaaaaaaaaat*?'

'I'll marry him myself.'

'Sibyl, you can't marry a dog!'

'Why not? It's not a real marriage. It's just television, remember? It'll be the highest rating wedding ever. What do we have to lose? Besides, he's kind of cute.'

'Oh, isn't that sweet,' Selby thought. 'I could give her a big kiss for that!'

And so it was that the bit at the beginning of this story happened and, what's more, Selby found himself on the Honeymoon Cruise of a Lifetime. It was as if he and Sibyl had the whole ship to themselves — well, to themselves and Gus the producer, the 'Mix 'n' Match Marriage' crew and a couple of hundred other passengers.

Selby was having the time of his life. During the daytime, he lazed in his deckchair beside Sibyl as the ship glided across the blue water. The camera crew took pictures of the two of them having lunch together in the dining room.

'You are an amazing dog, Selby,' Sibyl said to him one day. 'You're so friendly. You never misbehave the way some dogs do. It's as if you understand everything I say.'

'I do, I do, Sibyl,' Selby said, but of course he only said it in his head — he didn't say it out loud.

'We even like the same sort of food. I was amazed when you got stuck into those peanut prawns last night.'

'They were fantastic!' Selby thought. 'Almost as good as the ones from The Spicy Onion Restaurant back in Bogusville.'

'The TV crew loved it when you started moving around to that salsa music on the dance floor last night. It's almost as though you're part human. That's very odd, isn't it?'

'I am and it certainly is,' Selby thought.

On the door of Sibyl's cabin there was a big heart that said 'Selby & Sibyl'. Inside, Selby slept on his mat on the floor while Sibyl lay in bed looking out the porthole at the stars.

'You know, Selby, I've been to hundreds and hundreds of weddings and I've met lots and lots of men but I've never found Mr Perfect. But, as far as I'm concerned, you are Mr Perfect and you and I have the best friendship ever.'

'I agree, Sibs,' Selby thought, as he drifted off to sleep. 'I only wish this honeymoon thing could go on forever. Of course I'd (yawn) miss (yawn) the Trifles (yawn) if it did.'

And if everything was perfect (the way it sometimes is in Selby's stories), it was all about to change the very next day.

'Excuse me, young lady,' a charming voice said, 'but this dog of yours must be the most intelligent dog I've ever seen.'

Selby looked up from his deckchair to see a

very handsome man looking down at him and Sibyl.

'I beg your pardon?' Sibyl said, smiling up at the man.

'He not only picked up a scone in his paw but he spread butter and jam on it before eating it.'

'Selby did that?'

'Yes, indeed. A remarkable dog. And what a wonderful name. Selby. Allow me to introduce myself. I am Prince Pierre de Terre. But please just call me Pierre.'

'I am charmed to meet you, Pierre. I'm Sibyl.'

The man leaned down and lowered his voice to a whisper.

'Who is that person over there with the television camera?'

'Oh, that's Gus, my producer,' Sibyl said. 'I work for a television show called "Mix 'n' Match Marriage" and he's filming me for the show.'

'And are you married?' the prince asked.

'Yes, I just married Selby here and we're on our honeymoon.'

'You married a dog?'

'We're not really married,' Sibyl said.

'You mean it's not legal?'

'Hey, hang on, buster!' Selby thought. 'Two's company but three's a crowd around here.'

'No, of course not,' Sibyl said, smiling sweetly.

'But you are so lucky to have someone — even a dog,' Prince Pierre said. 'Sadly, my wife passed away last year. Since then, I've just been cruising around the world and giving away my money.'

'You're giving your money away?'

'Yes. You see, I've been very rich all my life and I know that money doesn't matter. The only thing that really matters is love.'

'But won't you be poor if you give away all your money?'

'That could never happen. I might have to sell one of the family castles but I have more money than I can give away in my whole lifetime,' the prince said. 'Would you and the wonderful Selby like to join me for dinner tonight?'

'Wonderful?' Selby thought. 'I think I'm getting to like this dude.'

'That would be lovely. Of course, Gus will have to be there with his camera taking pictures of us from time to time. Sorry, but it's part of my job.'

'I understand completely,' the prince said, bowing deeply.

That night, Selby, Sibyl and the prince had dinner in the dining room. Afterwards, Selby watched as Sibyl and Prince Pierre de Terre danced long into the night.

'If only I could dance like that,' Selby thought, 'holding Sibyl in my paws. Oh well, I guess I'm happy for Sibyl. He's not a bad bloke for a prince.'

Night after night, the couple dined and danced and talked. And when they'd finished talking, they talked some more.

One night, very late, there was a knock at Selby and Sibyl's door.

'Pssssst! It's me, Gus.'

Sibyl opened the door.

'Sibyl, you're brilliant!' Gus said. 'More people watched the show about you and Selby getting married than ever before.'

'What did I tell you?' Sibyl said.

'You were right. And for our next show we're going to do even better. We'll show the film I've taken of you and Selby on the cruise. Then we'll show you meeting the count.'

'He's a prince.'

'Whatever. And then we'll show you getting married to him right here on the ship.'

'I beg your pardon?'

'Oh, come on, you love him, don't you?'

'I *like* him but —'

'But nothing. You love him and he loves you and you're about to get engaged.'

'We are?'

'Yes. He's just asked the captain to do the wedding ceremony. Ships' captains can marry people, you know.'

'Oh, Gus, I do like him — a lot — but I can't marry someone when I'm already on my honeymoon with someone else.'

'What are you talking about? Selby's not a someone, he's a some*thing*. He's a dog, for pity's sake.'

'Now, hang on,' Selby thought. 'What's wrong with being a dog?'

'I'm sorry,' Sibyl said, 'but I wouldn't feel

right about it. And I don't think people who watch the show would, either.'

'You're wrong, Sibyl. Do it for your old friend Gus. Please?'

'No.'

'Good on you, Sibs,' Selby thought.

That night, Selby couldn't stop thinking about Sibyl and Pierre.

'He's so handsome and she's so beautiful,' he thought. 'And I think they really love each other. I'm sorry that I'm kinda in the way here, but hey ...'

The next morning, as Sibyl and Selby were walking around the deck, Prince Pierre de Terre came running.

'Sibyl dearest,' he said, falling to one knee, 'I love you. Do you love me?'

'Oh yes, *yes*! darling Pierre,' she gasped.

'Then will you marry me right here on the ship — today?'

'You must understand something, darling Pierre,' Sibyl said. 'I do love you but it wouldn't be right to marry you while I'm on my honeymoon with Selby.'

'That's right, Principoo,' Selby thought.

The prince got to his feet and looked down at Selby.

'But he's a dog.'

'Yes, I know that.'

'Yeah, so buzz off,' Selby thought. 'Suddenly I don't like this guy again.'

The prince threw up his hands.

'I understand, Sibyl,' he said. 'I don't want to upset you.'

'That's very nice of you,' Sibyl said.

After the prince had left, Selby went out for a walk around the deck. He saw the prince leaning against the railing.

'Hello, Selby, old boy,' Prince Pierre said in a slightly slimy voice. 'Well, my charm didn't quite work today, did it? But don't worry, it always works in the end. She'll agree to marry me sooner or later and then I'll get my hands on all that money of hers.'

'Oh no,' Selby thought. 'This Prince Smarmy is up to no good! I've got to warn Sibyl before it's too late!'

That evening, when Selby and Sibyl were alone in their cabin, he tried to warn her.

'Sibyl, *beware* of Prince Pierre de Terre. He

might seem like a nice guy but he's a sneak, and he's after your money. Don't marry him!'

Of course, Selby didn't say this — he secretly wrote it on a piece of paper. Then, just as he was about to slip it into an envelope, there was a knock at the door. Selby quickly stuffed the note into his mouth instead.

'Pierre, darling!' Sibyl cried, giving the prince a big hug. 'I'm so sorry about our disagreement today.'

'That's all right, darling. I understand. I just came to see if it would be okay to take Selby for a walk. He isn't getting enough exercise.'

'Thank you so much, Pierre,' Sibyl said. 'How thoughtful of you. Here's his leash.'

'Hey, I don't think I like the sound of this,' Selby thought.

Pierre led Selby up some stairs to the top deck. The moon shone in the black of the sea below.

'She'll be sad at first,' the prince said. 'But she'll get over it.'

'What is this guy talking about? What's she going to get over?'

Prince Pierre picked Selby up in his arms and patted him.

'It's not going to work, old boy,' Selby thought. 'You can be as nice to me as you want but I know what you're really like.'

'The thing is, Selby, no one can be married to a dead person. Or a dead dog, for that matter.'

'Yeah,' Selby thought, 'but I'm not dead and I don't expect to be dead for a long long time. Hey! What's he doing! He's lifting me over the railing! He's looking around to make sure no one's looking! He's —'

'Stop that!' Selby screamed in plain English (and, as he did so, the note flew out of his mouth and into the wind).

Prince Pierre stopped.

'You talked!'

'Of course I talked! Now put me down or I'll bite you into next week!'

But before either the prince or Selby could think to blink, the ship suddenly rolled and Selby found himself falling.

'Heeeeeeeeeeellllllllllllllppppppppppp!!!!!!!!!!' he screamed.

And that was the last sound from Selby as he plunged towards the icy depths.

* * *

Selby lay in the cold at the bottom of the sea, thinking about his wonderful life with the Trifles when he was alive.

'Why oh why did I ever get married?' he asked himself. 'I should have just bitten Sibyl the same way Posy bit Hamish, then none of this would have happened. And now Sibyl will marry that awful prince and he'll be horrible to her. If only I'd talked to her when I had a chance, I could have warned her.'

Over the sound of the roar of the sea, Selby heard sobbing.

'How could this have happened, darling?'

'That's Sibyl's voice!' he thought.

'It was terrible,' the prince said. 'He broke away from me. He started running and the next thing I knew he'd jumped off the side.'

'Whoa!' Selby thought. 'That's not what happened. Don't listen to him, Sibs!'

'But don't worry, darling. The first thing we'll do when we get married is get another dog just like Selby.'

'You'll never find another dog like me, you dog-murdering fiend,' Selby thought. 'Oh why did I let him kill me? And why can I hear everything they're saying? And what's this thing poking into my back?'

Selby opened his eyes and looked around in the dark, straining to see anything.

'Wait just a minute,' he thought. 'What's this? It feels like canvas. Hey, what do you know? I'm alive! I'm not at the bottom of the sea! I'm on top of a lifeboat! I didn't drown! I'm not dead any more!'

The ship rolled again and Selby clung to the top of the lifeboat. He climbed in under the cover.

'I think I'd better stay in here before I fall off and really drown. And, I'll tell you what, I'm going to hide till this cruise is over. I'm not taking any chances with that poncy prince.'

Selby hid in the lifeboat and drank the emergency water and ate the emergency biscuits. And all the while he wondered how he could secretly warn Sibyl about the prince. Suddenly he heard the sound of 'The Wedding March'.

'Oh, no!' he cried. 'She's going to marry him after all! How will I stop her?!'

In the ship's ballroom, all the passengers were gathered to watch the wedding of Sibyl Sweetie to Prince Pierre de Terre, while millions of people around the world watched on TV.

The captain, in his best white uniform, stood in front of the couple and began the wedding service as a small furry creature crept into the the ballroom through the back.

'If anyone knows of any reason why this wedding should not go ahead,' the captain said, 'speak now or forever hold your peace.'

There was a moment's silence and then ...

'Stop the wedding!' a voice cried out. 'They can't get married! He's already married!'

'Already married?' the captain said. 'Who said that?'

'I did,' the voice said, stepping forward.

'You? First Mate Alonzo?' (Because, you see, it wasn't Selby after all who spoke.) 'How do you know he's already married?'

'I ran a check on him. His name isn't Prince Pierre or Prince anything. His real name is Peter Grimes and he marries women for their money then runs off. He's still married to fifteen women.'

'Why, you horrid lying sneak!' Sibyl screamed, slapping him across the face. 'Oh, look!' she cried, racing down the aisle and picking Selby up. 'Selby's not dead, after all! Oh, you darling little dog. You are the dearest, most wonderful dog in the world.'

'And you're pretty okay yourself,' Selby thought.

And that's pretty much the end of the story. The ship docked that day and the Trifles were there to meet Selby and take him home to Bogusville. 'Mix 'n' Match Marriage' was watched by more people than ever and Sibyl got a big pay rise. Peter Grimes was taken away by the police and put in jail.

But you may want to know how it was that the First Mate found out about the prince.

'I found a soggy note stuck to the deck,' the First Mate explained. 'It wasn't signed and it looked like a child's writing. It said the prince was after Sibyl's money, so I thought I'd check it out. I'm glad I did.'

'And boy, am I glad he did, too,' Selby thought, as a slight doggy smile crept across his lips.

SELBY MEETS THE TRIPLE TERROR

'Melanie Mildew just phoned,' Mrs Trifle said. 'She wants us to meet her out at Gumboot Mountain. Apparently there's a big problem. She says we both have to go immediately so she can show us something.'

'Did she say what sort of problem it is?' Dr Trifle asked.

'No. She said she'd explain when we got there.'

'But we have to look after Willy and Billy this afternoon. We can't leave them here by themselves.'

'Willy and Billy?! Yikes,' Selby thought, 'if those super-brats are coming, I'm out of here!'

'They won't be by themselves,' Mrs Trifle said, 'because Jetty is bringing Cindy, Mindy and Lindy, as well. The girls can look after the boys.'

'Who are Cindy, Mindy and Lindy?'

'You know — the triplets. You haven't met them before but they're our nieces. Well, they're not exactly nieces, they're my uncle's cousin's brother-in-law's stepson's daughters, but I think of them as nieces. They go to SLC in the city but they're staying with Jetty for the weekend.'

'SLC? Is that a school?'

'Yes, the whole name is St Lucre's College for Polite Young Ladies,' Mrs Trifle explained. 'It's the most expensive school in the country. I haven't seen the girls since they were two but I'm sure they're absolutely lovely. Jetty says that Willy and Billy always behave themselves when the girls are around.'

'Who is she kidding? Willy and Billy? Behave? They wouldn't know the meaning of the word,' Selby thought. 'No little girls could ever be able to keep those monsters under control. This I've got to see.'

Minutes later, Aunt Jetty's car stopped outside. And, within a moment, Willy and Billy were running around the house hitting each other with their cricket bats. Selby had quietly climbed on top of a kitchen cabinet and was peeking over the edge.

'*Ow*! He hit me!' Billy screamed.

'He hit me too!' Willy screamed back. 'I'm going to get him!'

'You'll do nothing of the sort!' Mrs Trifle said. 'Stop hitting each other this instant!'

Willy and Billy kept running and screaming and were still bashing each other with their bats when the three girls came quietly into the room.

'Ahem,' Cindy said, clearing her throat. 'Boys, will you please stop what you're doing right now?'

At the sweet sound of Cindy's voice, Willy and Billy stopped in their tracks and dropped their bats. Selby was surprised to see fear on the boys' faces.

'Y-Yes, C-C-Cindy,' Willy said. 'I'll do anything you say.'

'Me too,' Billy said.

'What's going on here?' Selby wondered.

'Remember,' Cindy added, 'we're guests in the Trifles' house so you will both have to behave.'

'We will. Honest,' the boys said together.

'All right then,' said Mindy. 'That way nothing will get broken.'

'And neither of you will be hurt,' Lindy added.

'I can't believe it!' Selby thought. 'Those monsters are as tame as kittens. It's got to be an act. They just have to be faking.'

'That's amazing,' Mrs Trifle said. 'You certainly are good with the boys. We were a little worried about leaving you here all by yourselves.'

'There's nothing to worry about, Auntie,' Cindy said. Then she turned to her sisters. 'Say it, girls!'

The girls stood in a row with their hands neatly folded in front of them as they chanted, 'We're neat. We're sweet. And we're as cute as cute can be.' They then burst into giggles.

'Don't worry about Willy and Billy,' Mindy said. 'I'm sure they'll be as good as gold.'

'I hope so,' Mrs Trifle said, turning to the boys, 'because if you boys are naughty then you're going to be in big trouble when we get back. Do you understand?'

'Yes, Auntie,' Willy and Billy said.

'I can't believe this,' Selby thought. 'Willy and Billy being good? What planet am I on?'

No sooner had the Trifles driven off than Melanie Mildew arrived at the door with a group of council workers.

'I'm sorry but the Trifles are out,' Cindy said.

'We know,' Melanie said. 'We're the ones who tricked them into leaving the house. You see, Mrs Trifle has been the mayor of Bogusville for twenty-one years today and we want to give her a surprise party.'

'How exciting,' Mindy said. 'Come in.'

Very soon, people were rushing everywhere. They were setting up tables and chairs and putting out plates of food. Melanie hung a huge banner in the loungeroom that said,

HAPPY ANNIVERSARY, MAYOR TRIFLE!

'What a wonderful surprise!' Selby thought as he watched from his hiding place on top of the cabinet. 'Mrs Trifle's going to be so happy. And that food smells absolutely scrummy. There's even a cake that says "HAPPY 21st ANNIVERSARY" . She'll *love* that.'

'Okay,' Melanie said when everything was set up. 'We've got to leave now to get dressed and organise the band.' She turned to Willy and Billy. 'Don't touch anything — do you understand?'

'We won't,' the boys said.

'We'll keep an eye on them,' said Lindy. 'We promise they won't touch a thing.'

And, with that, Melanie Mildew and the other council workers left.

'Well well well, girls,' Cindy said when the front door closed and they were alone again. 'Look at all the lovely food.'

'Yes, it looks fantastic,' Mindy said.

Lindy picked up a little sandwich. 'I wonder if it tastes as good as it looks,' she said.

'Don't eat it!' Willy cried. 'You promised!'

'We only promised that *you boys* wouldn't touch the food, didn't we, girls?' Cindy said.

'That's the way I remember it,' Mindy said, taking a bite out of a little sausage.

'No, no, no!' Billy howled. 'We'll get in trouble!'

'Oh, puuuuleez,' Mindy said, grabbing a handful of potato chips. 'You're making me cry.'

Willy grabbed her arm but she pushed him against a table, spilling fruit punch all over the floor.

'Go for it, girls!' Cindy cried as she knocked Billy out of the way. 'Let's party!'

'I can't believe this!' Selby thought. 'Those sweet little innocent girls are worse than Willy and Billy. They're dreadful! They're going to ruin Mrs Trifle's surprise party!'

For the next few minutes the girls feasted on everything in sight, sometimes taking only a bite or two out of scones and sandwiches and then putting them back on the plates.

Willy and Billy looked on silently with tears streaming down their faces.

'What's the matter with you two?' Cindy demanded.

'We're going to be in big big trouble,' Willy bawled.

'Mum won't let us go out for a year,' Billy whimpered.

'But you haven't done anything wrong,' Cindy said. 'They look completely innocent, don't they, girls?'

'They certainly do,' Lindy said.

'But we'll soon fix that!' Mindy said as she and her sisters held the boys down and smeared their faces with chocolate.

'Goodness gracious,' Cindy said. 'Now they don't look so innocent, after all. Come on, girls! Let's party some more!'

Food flew everywhere. Spoonfuls of dip hit the ceiling, pies smashed against the walls, sandwiches were squashed into the carpet. Willy and Billy huddled in the corner sobbing while the girls shook up cans of drink and sprayed them everywhere.

And, just when Selby thought they couldn't do any more damage, Mindy said, 'Aren't we forgetting something, girls?' and picked up the cake.

'That's it!' Selby thought. 'That's the last straw! I don't mind Willy and Billy getting into trouble — they've certainly made my life a misery 🐾 — but I can't let these terrible triplets ruin Mrs Trifle's anniversary cake! I can't just lie here quietly! I've got to say something!'

Selby opened his mouth to yell, 'No, no, not the cake!' but, just at that instant, it flew up into the air, filling his mouth and splattering against the ceiling.

'Good shot!' Cindy yelled. 'You hit the dog! What's that dog doing up there, anyway?'

The force of the flying cake knocked Selby off balance and sent him crashing to the floor.

'That's that stink-face doggy!' Willy yelled. 'He knows how to talk!'

'Yeah, he does,' Billy agreed. 'Hey, Willy, he can tell Auntie we didn't do anything.'

'Sure, he can,' Lindy laughed. 'Come along, girls, let's get out of here. I can't stand this mess.'

'Okay,' Cindy said. 'But we've got to be back to see what the Trifles do to those naughty little boys.'

'Yeah,' said Mindy. 'Boys are such messy little animals.'

🐾 Paw note: If you want to see how horrible Willy and Billy have been to me, read the story 'Animal Angels' in the book Selby Scrambled. S

Selby and Willy and Billy watched the girls go skipping down the street.

'You have to tell Auntie and Uncle we didn't do it,' Willy said to Selby.

'Yeah, you have to,' Billy said. 'Please, doggy? We'll be really really nice to you.'

Selby washed the cake off his face in the kitchen sink and stood silently, thinking.

'I'm not going to do it,' he thought. 'I can't give away my secret just for Willy and Billy. I mean, they've been horrible to me all my life!'

'You have to tell,' Willy begged. '*Pleeeeeeease*!'

Selby shook his head.

'But we didn't do nothin'!' Billy wailed.

'They're right, of course,' Selby thought. 'And they probably deserve everything they're going to get for all the terrible things they've done to me. But I feel sorry for Mrs Trifle. Her party is completely ruined and her house is a mess.'

'Please, doggy, please,' Willy said, getting down on his knees. 'I'm begging you.'

Selby smiled a small doggy smile.

'Okay,' he said.

'Are you gonna talk?' Billy asked. 'Are you gonna tell them?'

'No,' Selby said. 'I'm not going to tell anyone anything.'

'Then what are you going to do?'

'You mean, what are *we* going to do,' Selby said. 'I'm going to tell you what to do and you're going to do exactly as I say. Do you understand?'

'Okay, Mr Doggy,' Willy said.

'Good. Then close the curtains, lock the doors and let's get started. First of all, put those tablecloths in the washing machine. Take off your clothes and put them in there too.'

'But then we'll be in the nuddy,' Willy said.

'Yeah, we can't clean up when we're in the nuddy,' Billy said.

'Sorry, guys, but I'm making the rules around here. Hurry up now!'

Selby opened a recipe book and, for the next half-hour, he mixed a cake and put it in the oven. Meanwhile, Willy and Billy threw away the spoiled food and cleaned the walls and ceiling. Selby got lots of biscuits out of the cupboard and put bits of cheese on them and then found a loaf of bread and made sandwiches. When the washing machine finished, the clothes and tablecloths went into the dryer. Soon, Willy and Billy were dressed and everything looked neat and tidy.

Selby got the cake out of the oven.

'Open the curtains in the loungeroom now and keep an eye out,' Selby said, 'while I put the icing on the cake.'

Selby was just squeezing the icing writing onto the cake when Willy cried, 'It's them! Cindy and them are back!'

'Whatever you do, don't let them in,' Selby said. 'Keep the front door locked till the Trifles get here.'

Suddenly there was loud knocking.

'Open up, you boys!' Cindy yelled. 'Let us in!'

'Don't do it,' Selby said, as he finished the writing on the cake. 'Billy!' he whispered. 'Come over here.'

Billy placed the cake neatly on the table.

'Good work, guys,' Selby said. 'It looks almost the same as it was before the girls got to it.'

'Hey, where have they gone?' Willy asked, unlocking the front door and stepping outside. 'They went away.'

Selby was suddenly aware of three little innocent-looking figures coming in through the back door.

'Weeee're baaaaack,' Cindy sang. 'You silly boys. You forgot to lock the back door, didn't you?'

'Well! Will you have a look at this,' Mindy said. 'The boys have cleaned everything up and have got another surprise party ready.'

'I think it's time we gave them another surprise,' Lindy said.

Each of the girls picked up a plate of food and was about to throw it when Willy screamed, 'Noooooooooooooooo!'

And they still would have thrown the plates if they hadn't seen the Trifles' car pulling into the driveway.

'Quickly, girls!' Cindy whispered. 'The Trifles are back! One, two, three, *throw*!'

In that instant, before the girls could hurl their plates of food into the air, a jumble of letters tumbled around in Selby's head like Scrabble squares in a cyclone as his mouth tried to make the right words. Then, in a split second, his lips moved and out came a cry that sounded like, '*Don't you dare do that*!'

The girls stopped and spun around.

'That dog talked!' Cindy cried.

'Yeah, he did!' Lindy cried.

'I heard it too!' Mindy cried.

Suddenly the door flew open and in came the Trifles followed by Melanie Mildew and the council workers.

'What is this?!' Mrs Trifle gasped. 'My goodness! It's a party — for me!'

'Surprise! Surprise!' Melanie yelled and everyone cheered and clapped.

'Melanie!' Mrs Trifle said, wagging her finger. 'You're a naughty girl. You tricked us. But what a lovely surprise.'

The three girls were still holding the plates they'd been about to throw. Cindy stepped forward and very politely said, 'Anyone care for a sandwich?'

'Or a sausage?' Lindy said sweetly.

'Or a biscuit?' Mindy said even more sweetly.

'Oh, *yes*,' Mrs Trifle said, taking some food from Cindy's plate. 'Thank you very much.'

'And thanks for looking after things while we were out,' Dr Trifle said.

'You're very welcome, Uncle,' Cindy said, turning to her sisters. 'What do we say, girls?'

The girls put a finger to their chins and chanted, 'We're neat. We're sweet. And we're as cute as cute can be,' before bursting into giggles.

'Oh that's so cute!' said Mrs Trifle.

'Pardon me while I vomit,' Selby thought.

'And look at that beautiful cake,' Dr Trifle said. 'Hmmm, there's only one thing wrong.'

'Wrong?' Mrs Trifle said. 'What's wrong?'

'Someone's left one of the Ns out of the word *anniversary*.'

Willy and Billy looked around at Selby.

'Hey,' Selby thought, and he gave the slightest of slight shrugs. 'Nobody's perfect. Not even me.'

SELBY'S SHADOW

'I've come up with something to make people invisible,' Dr Trifle said.

'Invisible?' thought Selby , just waking up from his nap.

'Invisible?' Mrs Trifle asked. 'Who would want to be invisible?'

'Lots of people. Soldiers, for example. That way, the enemy couldn't see them.'

'But they already have that camel clothing thingy to make them invisible.'

'I think you mean *camouflage* clothing.'

> 🐾 Paw note: Not that again! Read my story 'See-Through Selby' in the book Selby's Shemozzle.

S

'Yes, those shirts and pants with the blotches all over them.'

'There's a problem with them,' Dr Trifle said. 'They don't get rid of the shadows. Which is how enemy aircraft find soldiers. They use cameras and computers to look for shadows. If they see a shadow where a shadow shouldn't be then they know there's a soldier there. But I think I know how to make the shadows disappear.'

'Speaking of shadows,' Mrs Trifle said, 'that reminds me of Mr Sombra.'

'Who's Mr Sombra?'

'He's a puppeteer. He wants to do his Magic Shadow Show at the school. I'm having a look at it first to see if it's good enough.'

'What sort of a shadow show is it?' Dr Trifle asked.

'He makes shadows with his hands. He's supposed to be very good at it. We'll see because here he comes now,' Mrs Trifle said, glancing out the window.

Selby jumped to his feet as an old van screeched to a stop outside the house. Out hopped a strange little man carrying a big suitcase.

'Hello, Mrs Mayor and Mrs Mayor's Husband,' he said, bowing deeply as he came through the door. 'I am Mr Sombra. I am so happy to present Mr Sombra's Magic Shadow Show. Oh, look at the pretty dog,' he added, bowing to Selby too.

'I wish he'd said handsome,' Selby thought, 'but pretty will do.'

'A moment, please, Mrs Mayor and Mrs Mayor's Husband and Mrs Mayor's Doggy. I get myself ready very soon now.'

Selby and the Trifles watched as Mr Sombra set up a white screen with a spotlight behind it.

'Now you watch Magic Shadow Show,' he said, ducking behind the screen. 'This story called *Mooka-Mooka, Very Smart Bird and Big Bad Monster.*'

Suddenly the shadow of a bird with a long beak appeared on the screen. The bird was sitting on a branch. Mr Sombra made chirping and tweeting sounds.

'This guy's good,' Selby thought. 'It looks and sounds just like a real bird.'

The bird's wings started flapping and soon it was flying through the air.

'*Long ago,*' Mr Sombra said, '*there was very smart bird named Mooka-Mooka. He is flying flying flying. He look down on little town of . . . Bogusville.*'

'Oh, that's nice,' Mrs Trifle said. 'The kids will love that.'

'*But Mooka-Mooka see all the animals in Bogusville is very sad,*' Mr Sombra said. '*The rabbits is sad . . .*'

A shadow of a rabbit appeared in the middle of the screen. It hopped and hopped, getting bigger and bigger till it filled the screen.

'*The kangaroos is sad . . .*'

The rabbit disappeared and two kangaroos hopped towards each other from either side of the screen.

'This guy is brilliant!' Selby thought. 'One hand for each kangaroo — and they look so real!'

The kangaroos hugged each other and Mr Sombra made sobbing sounds.

Mrs Trifle giggled.

'No laughing, please!' Mr Sombra said sharply. 'This not funny! Very sad.'

'I'm terribly sorry,' Mrs Trifle said.

'*The cows is sad. And the horses is sad. Even the cheeps is sad.*'

Selby watched in amazement as the cows turned into horses and then sheep.

'*And the pipples is sad too,*' Mr Sombra said.

The sheep turned into people.

'*The pipples is sad because they is scared of . . . the monster! The monster is eating up all the animals. First he eat the bunny rabbits . . .*'

'That's horrible!' Mrs Trifle said.

'You wait,' Mr Sombra said. 'It get more horrible now. *Then the monster eat one cow. Then he eat kangaroo. Then more kangaroo. Then he eat all the cheeps.*'

One by one, the shadow monster ate the animals, burping after each one.

'Sheesh!' thought Selby. 'This story is giving me the creeps.'

'*He is very hungry monster. End of story,*' Mr Sombra said. 'You like?'

'I'm not sure,' Mrs Trifle said. 'Don't the people kill the monster in the end?'

'Oh, I forget,' Mr Sombra said. '*Then monster eat the lady and he eat the man too. He eat all the pipples up and eat up Mooka-Mooka very smart bird. Munch munch munch. Very nice.'*

'Goodness me!' Mrs Trifle exclaimed. 'Shouldn't there be a happy ending?'

'Happy endings is always boring,' Mr Sombra said. 'My show different.'

'Do you have any other stories you could tell?' Mrs Trifle asked.

'Okay, I have story called *Nice Boy and Terrible Little Girl*. In the end, she chop his head off. Ha ha! Very funny one. And I have *Old Lady Who Work Very Hard Then Die*. A train run over her. I do very good train. *Choo choo choo choo. Woo Woo!'*

'Mr Sombra,' Mrs Trifle said, 'your shadows are very good but I really don't think your show is right for the children of Bogusville.'

'Is stupid!' Mr Sombra said, packing up his things. 'I don't like happy story. I don't like this Bogusville!'

'I'm terribly sorry,' Mrs Trifle said.

'I curse this town!' Mr Sombra said, tripping over Selby as he headed for the door. 'Out of my way, stupid dog! I put a curse on you, too!'

And, within a minute, Mr Sombra's van had sped off down the street.

'That man is not a happy man,' Dr Trifle said.

'I'm glad I saw the show first,' Mrs Trifle said. 'I think those stories would really have upset the kids.'

'You know, I don't think Bogusville has ever had a curse put on it before,' Dr Trifle said.

'No, I don't think it has,' Mrs Trifle agreed. 'Do you think curses work?'

'Of course not,' Dr Trifle said.

'I hope you're right,' Mrs Trifle said. 'Poor old Selby. He's got a curse on him now, as well.'

'Curse schmurse,' Selby thought. 'I don't believe in curses. I laugh at curses. Ha ha ha! That Mr Sombra doesn't worry me a bit.'

That night, Selby had a nightmare about Mr Sombra.

'No! Don't put a curse on me, please!' he screamed in his dream. 'I'll do anything you say!'

After a terrible night's sleep, he woke up to see the Trifles staring down at him.

'Do you think it worked?' Mrs Trifle asked.

'Hard to tell,' said Dr Trifle. 'I think we'll just have to wait and see.'

'Wait? Wait for what?' Selby thought. 'What are they talking about? What are they looking at me like that for? Surely they don't think there's a curse on me.'

Selby munched a Dry-Mouth Dog Biscuit as the Trifles watched.

'Something about him does look . . . different,' Mrs Trifle said.

'Yes, maybe it is working, after all.'

'Cut it out, you guys,' Selby thought. (He didn't say it, he only thought it.) 'You're making me nervous. I'm getting out of here.'

Selby set out for a long walk.

'The flies are terrible,' he said to himself as he shook dozens of them off his back. 'They're never this bad. Hey, and look! The floral clock 🐾 has stopped. And it stopped exactly at midnight! Spooky dooky.'

Selby walked on as dark clouds gathered above the town. The wind picked up and a willy-willy swirled along the street, gathering up dust and pieces of paper. Selby clung to a lamp-post as the willy-willy passed by.

🐾 *Paw note: Bogusville has a wonderful clock made of flowers.*

S

'That was a close one!' he thought. 'It could have picked me right up and carried me off! This is getting scary. I'm going home where I'll be safe with the Trifles.'

Selby could feel the sweat running down his face as he headed for home.

'Hey! There's a big crowd at the sportsground,' he said, breaking into a run. 'There must be a cricket match on. I wonder who's playing. I can see the scoreboard now. Poshfield 174. Bogusville 2. We must have just gone in to bat. Poshfield is pathetic. We can beat 174 easily. Whoa,' he said, as he got closer. 'They're not playing cricket — they're playing soccer! One hundred and seventy-four is the highest soccer score ever! Mr Sombra's curse must be working!'

As the crowd started to leave the stadium, the sun came out. Selby saw a startled look on a little girl's face.

'Mummy, look!' she cried. 'That dog doesn't have a shadow!'

'What a strange thing to say,' the woman said. 'Good grief! You're right! He doesn't have a shadow!'

'What are they on about?' Selby thought. 'Is this a trick? Maybe the kid has worked out that the Selby in the books is me. Maybe she's trying to trick me into looking down at my shadow. Then, if I do, she'll know that I can understand people-talk. She'll know it's me, Selby, the only talking dog in Australia and, perhaps, the world. Well, I'm not going to look down.'

Selby walked faster, keeping his head held high. The girl and her mother were following him now.

'How does she know it's me?' Selby thought. 'Did I give away too many clues in my stories?'

'Look! Everyone look!' the little girl yelled. 'The doggy doesn't have a shadow!'

Everyone looked at Selby.

'Oh, no!' Selby thought. 'Get me out of here!'

Selby switched from a walk to a trot as people tried to catch up.

'The little girl is right!' a man cried. 'It's a shadowless dog!'

'He's some kind of devil dog!' a woman yelled. 'Look, everyone!'

Selby switched from a trot to a run and, as he did, he peeped over his nose towards the ground.

'My shadow! It's gone! The sun is out and they've all got shadows but I don't!' he thought. 'The curse is working!'

'Catch him!' someone yelled. 'I want a photo! Don't let him get away!'

'If they catch me, they'll send me off to a science laboratory to be studied!' Selby thought. 'My life will never be the same! And it's all because of that stupid Mr Sombra and his curse!'

Selby was running as fast as he could with the crowd gaining on him. Then, hearing the sound of a roaring car behind him, he shot off the road and through the trees.

'Hey! Bogusville Creek's up ahead!' he thought. 'I'll just dive in and swim across. That'll lose them.'

But, as he got to the creek, he suddenly remembered something.

'What am I thinking? I don't know how to swim! I've got to find another way across.'

Selby tore along the riverbank with the little girl close behind.

'Mummy! Mummy! He's slowing down. I'm going to catch him!'

'We'll see about that,' Selby thought as he ran along a branch that lay across the river. 'There are some things a dog can do that a little girl can't.'

Unfortunately, running across branches that stretch across fast-flowing creeks wasn't one of them. Not with a sure-footed little girl pounding along behind him.

'I'm (gasp) almost (gasp) there but she's (gasp) making the branch bounce,' Selby thought. 'This isn't a tree branch — it's a trampoline!'

And, in that instant, Selby bounced up into the air, then did a half flip, three turns and a forward roll into the raging creek.

'Help!' he cried out in plain English — knowing that he was giving away his secret forever. 'I can't swim! Somebody save me!'

Selby could have saved his breath. In fact, Selby *should* have saved his breath because when he yelled he was deep underwater. Not only could no one hear him but his lungs were filling with water.

He bobbed to the surface, this time yelling out, 'I'm drowning!' But all that came out was a rush of water followed by gasping and gurgling.

'The doggy can't swim!' the little girl yelled, as Selby was swept away in the swirling water.

'Nonsense!' her mother said. 'Every dog can swim.'

'But this one can't! He's drowning!'

Without a second thought, the little girl dived into the creek, grabbed Selby by the collar and dragged him to shore.

Selby lay on the grass coughing and spluttering in the warm sun. Just then, Bogusville's two police officers, Sergeant Short and Constable Long, made their way through the crowd.

'Why, that's Selby, Mayor Trifle's dog,' Sergeant Short said. 'What's wrong with him?'

'He almost drowned but I saved him,' the little girl said. 'And guess what? He doesn't have a shadow.'

'He what?' Constable Long said.

'It's true,' the girl's mother said. 'He doesn't have a shadow. It's really weird.'

The police officers looked down at Selby.

'This is it,' Selby thought. 'Selby's curse. The shadowless dog. I'm a freak — and it's all Mr Sombra's fault.'

'He's got a shadow,' Sergeant Short said, pointing. 'Look.'

Everyone looked, even Selby.

'So I do,' Selby thought. 'I've got my shadow back! The curse has lifted! I'm not a freak any more! Oh joy, oh joy!'

When Selby was safely at home with the Trifles, his mind turned again to the curse.

'I was silly. I thought Bogusville was filling up with flies,' he thought. 'It *always* fills up with flies at this time of year. And there are willy-willies all the time in summer. And the clock hands stopping at midnight. That was the silliest thing of all. Both hands were pointing to twelve. It could have stopped at mid*day*, not mid*night*. Come to think of it, when I passed the clock it *was* midday. The hands of the clock hadn't stopped at all. The only thing I can't figure out is that shadow business.'

'It's a mystery,' Dr Trifle said to Mrs Trifle. 'I sprayed my newly-invented ShadeAway all over

Selby this morning when he was sleeping but it obviously doesn't work.'

'How do you know?'

'Because I saw him come back from his walk and his shadow was trotting right alongside him. It was there all right. My invention is useless.'

'Hmmm,' Mrs Trifle said. 'I guess you're right. You don't suppose it got washed off, do you?'

'Washed off? Impossible. It hasn't rained for ages. Look out there — it's a beautiful sunny day.'

'It certainly is,' Selby thought. 'Without a shadow of doubt. A shadow of a doubt? What am I saying?'

I'M NOT A TROTTER OR A PACER

by Selby Trifle

I'm not a trotter or a pacer,
Or any other kind of racer.
To tell the truth I'm not so fast,
I only ever come dead last.

But there's a race I'd love to win,
If only they would let me in.
Yes I would set a cracking pace,
If I could join the *human* race.

THE MOVIE MAGIC OF JIGSAW JABBAR

'Who's that strange-looking boy?' Dr Trifle said to Mrs Trifle.

It was Saturday morning and the Trifles were strolling through Bogusville with Selby.

'Which one?'

'The barefoot one wearing a torn T-shirt and pants that are all ragged and falling down. He must be very poor. Do you think he'd let us buy him a belt?'

'I don't think he's poor,' Mrs Trifle said. 'That's the way young people dress these days. And he's not a boy — he's a young man named Jigsaw Jabbar. He's getting to be quite a famous fantasy film-maker.'

'He doesn't look old enough to be a famous anything,' Dr Trifle said. 'I wonder where he got that name — Jigsaw.'

'It's a nickname. His real name is Jabbar something-or-other. When he was ten, he was the world champion jigsaw puzzler. He could put a thousand-piece jigsaw puzzle together in two-and-a-half minutes. And that was with the picture side face-down so he could only see the back of the pieces.'

'Goodness me, I can't even do them right-side up. How do you know all this?'

'I said hello to him the other day and we had a nice chat. He's given up jigsaw puzzles and started making movies.'

'What sort of movies?'

'Those ones with knights and castles and people fighting weird monsters. You and I saw one on DVD. Remember a film called *Dragon Mist Enigma*? That was one of his.'

'He made that?!' Selby thought. 'That was brilliant! I loved all that stuff with fighting monsters.'

'He made that?' Dr Trifle said. 'I liked it but there was too much monster-fighting for me.'

'We also saw *Legions of the Fire King* and *Snow Dream Castle.*'

'I loved those films, too!' Selby thought. 'I can't believe he's actually here in Bogusville!'

'He's hired the Bogusville Bijou Movie Theatre to use as a studio,' Mrs Trifle continued. 'He's just finishing a movie in there right now.'

'He must have hundreds of people working for him,' Dr Trifle said. 'It's funny that I haven't seen more strangers around town.'

'I know,' Mrs Trifle said. 'I haven't seen any other strangers, either. They're probably working so hard that they never leave the theatre.'

'What I'd like to know is, if he's such a big-time film-maker, why isn't he working in Hollywood? Or New Zealand?'

'He said he likes the peace and quiet here. And he doesn't like people snooping around when he's making a movie. Bogusville people don't snoop around.'

'Maybe not,' Selby thought, 'but there's one Bogusville *dog* who does. I think I might just drop in to the Bogusville Bijou and have a squiz. I know what these movie sets are like. They'll be so busy that no one will even notice me 🐾.'

It was a silent dog that tiptoed out of the Trifle's house that afternoon and trotted down to the Bogusville Bijou. And it was a curious dog that climbed up a pile of boxes and in through a window at the back of the theatre.

'Hey, it's as quiet as a graveyard in here,' Selby thought. 'Where is everyone?'

A beam of light shone through a crack in the curtain. Selby moved slowly towards it.

'Who is it?' a voice demanded.

'Someone's heard me!' Selby thought.

'Yes, Harry, it's me, Jigsaw,' the voice said again.

'Phew,' Selby phewed. 'He's just talking on his mobile.'

🐾 *Paw note: I ought to know — I've made a movie myself. See the story 'Selby's Stardom' in the book* Selby's Stardom.

S

121

'Okay, okay,' Jigsaw said. 'Stop worrying. We're almost finished. Trust me. We've been working around the clock for the past four days. We haven't had a wink of sleep. I'll upload the film to you in about an hour. You can screen it as soon as I start uploading. The guys are working on a tiny technical problem with the last scene right now.'

Selby peeked out into the darkened theatre. There, in front of him, was the young man sitting alone in one of the seats. The theatre was completely empty except for him.

'Guys?' Selby thought. 'What guys is he talking about? Who's he kidding? There's nobody here but him.'

'What did you say, Harry?' Jigsaw went on. 'Don't worry. Just feed the movie reviewers some popcorn. Yes, I know how important they are. It'll be worth the wait. This movie will knock their socks off. Now let me get back to work, okay?'

Selby watched as Jigsaw Jabbar opened the laptop that he held on his knees. Suddenly the movie screen flickered. Selby made his way up the side aisle and parked himself on a seat behind Jigsaw.

'Hey, that's great!' Selby thought. 'The big movie screen is showing what he's doing on his laptop.'

Selby settled back into his seat as Jigsaw Jabbar fast-forwarded through the movie.

'Even when it's going really really fast, I can tell it's fantastic,' he thought.

Jigsaw stopped the action. He closed his eyes and leaned his head back. Suddenly he opened his eyes and jerked forward again.

'The poor guy is really tired,' Selby thought.

'Got to get through this,' Jigsaw said out loud. 'Got to make the last scene and the film will be finished.'

'*Make* the last scene?' Selby thought. 'Is he kidding? It takes weeks — or months — to do a scene in a movie. You've got to get the actors and they've got to learn their lines. And then there's the make-up people and the sets. What is it with this guy?'

Jigsaw typed something on the keyboard and then picked up a little microphone.

'Mountains,' he said.

Suddenly the outline of mountains appeared on the movie screen.

'Colour,' he said. 'Grays and browns. Jagged rocks. Tufts of grass. Snow on mountain peaks.'

Each time Jigsaw spoke, the picture changed, becoming more and more realistic.

'This guy's a genius!' Selby thought. 'He's invented a computer program that turns his words into movies. No wonder he can do everything himself. And no wonder he doesn't want anyone snooping around to find out his secret.'

'Mountains higher,' Jigsaw went on. 'Steeper. More cliffs. Waterfalls. Eagles in the sky. Stone castle on top of rocky peak. Six wooden towers on castle. One tower very tall.'

Jigsaw put his head in his hands.

'Wake up!' Selby thought. 'Come on, you can do it!'

Jigsaw slowly stretched his neck by turning his head from side to side.

'Sounds. Water and wind,' he said. 'Action.'

Suddenly the scene came alive. Eagles soared in the sky. Grass bent in the wind. Waterfalls streamed out of the rocks and into the valley below.

'Soldier style twenty-two B,' Jigsaw said. 'Body armour style three-six-seven J.'

A huge man with long black hair appeared. He was holding a club and a whip.

'Multiply soldier times six hundred.'

Suddenly there were six hundred warriors.

'Bows and arrows. Clubs. Whips. Spears. Selection twenty-three. Armour Selection four Q. Mix.'

'Wow!' Selby thought. 'This is the most fantastic computer program ever!'

'Lower drawbridge,' Jigsaw went on. 'Warriors into castle. Take up guard positions. Insert Princess Fairhair from Clipboard two-three-five.'

There in the middle of the screen was a beautiful young woman with long blonde hair.

'Princess into tall tower. Insert Army of Akrads from scene six-two-nine approaching on horseback. Play drumbeat. Start battle set-up fifteen and twenty-one. Action.'

Selby watched as a thousand dark figures poured through mountain passes riding their elephant-like beasts. The half-human, half-monster figures now filled the screen, their huge teeth dripping goo, their eyes blood red.

'Music continuity. Sequence ten minutes,' Jigsaw called out. 'Akrad attack on castle. Akrads winning for eight minutes. Princess Fairhair leads counter–attack. She and ten warriors survive. Credit roll. Wrap.'

Selby watched the final battle scene with his heart pounding in his chest. Jigsaw slumped forward, his chin resting on the seat in front of him.

As the credits began to roll, Selby couldn't stop himself. He clapped and cheered wildly.

'Wonderful!' he cried without thinking.

The boy-wizard film–maker turned in his seat.

'Who's there? What did you say?'

Selby sat silently, trying to look as innocent as a dog who had just yelled out in plain English could have looked.

'Hey! You're a dog!' Jigsaw exclaimed. 'Or am I just imagining you? Come here, boy. Come on. Here doggy doggy.'

'I'd better do what he says,' Selby thought as he trotted down the aisle and climbed up on the seat next to Jigsaw.

'Are you real?' Jigsaw asked, rubbing his eyes. 'You *look* real.'

Silence.

Jigsaw gave Selby a pat.

'And you *feel* real,' he said, 'so you must be real. But tell me you didn't say *wonderful*.'

More silence.

'Wonderful,' Jigsaw said, staring into Selby's eyes.

Selby opened his mouth.

'W-w-w-,' he started. And then he said, '*Woof*!'

'Yeah, I was hearing things,' Jigsaw said, leaning over and reading Selby's tag. 'Selby,' he said. 'Good name. If I were a dog, I'd like to be called Selby 🐾.'

Jigsaw's mobile started ringing but he didn't answer it.

'That'll be Harry and his film critics. I'm not going to answer it and I'm not going to upload the film to them. Sorry guys, but it's rubbish.'

'No, it's not,' Selby thought. 'It's great!'

'Boring boring boring,' Jigsaw mumbled. 'It's the same old thing. *Dragon Mist Enigma*, *Legions of the Fire King*, *Snow Dream Castle*, and now this

🐾 *Paw note: Of course my tag has my real name on it.*

S

128

one, *Myth Chaser*. They're all the same. I've made the same film four times.'

'I could see twenty of them and not be bored,' Selby thought.

'They always want you to do the same thing over and over again. I want to break out. I want to do something different for a change.'

'What does it take to make this guy happy?' Selby wondered. 'He's made some great films! He's famous!'

'Do you know what would make me happy?' Jigsaw said to Selby as if Selby could understand what he was saying (which he could). 'I'd be happy if I could make a happy movie with lots of singing and dancing in it.'

Jigsaw's mobile kept ringing.

'Oh, be quiet,' he said to it. 'Tell the movie reviewers to go home because they're not going to see this film. I'm going to delete the whole thing right now. And then (yawn) I'm going to (yawn) get some sleep.'

Selby watched in horror as Jigsaw's finger headed for the DELETE button.

'He doesn't know what he's doing!' Selby screamed in his brain.

'Don't do it!' Selby blurted out. 'You'll be sorry you did!'

But the last thing Jigsaw did before slumping back in his chair and falling into a deep sleep was to press the DELETE button. Soon he was dreaming of his film career; of this, his last movie; and thinking about the very furry DELETE button that he'd just pressed. A furry DELETE button with claws on it.

'Thank goodness,' Selby thought as he lifted the man's finger from the back of his paw. 'I saved the film. Now to send it. Let's see now . . .'

Selby searched the keyboard of the laptop and found a button that said UPLOAD and was just about to press it.

'Now hang on a tick,' he thought. 'What am I doing? I mean, I loved the film but Jigsaw didn't like it and it's *his* film. Who am I to send it? But, if I don't send it right now, it'll never get shown in theatres. And maybe he didn't like it because he was just too tired. If I delete it, he might wake up and wish he still had it.'

Selby rested his paw on the keyboard again. He looked at the boy-genius film-maker and shook his head.

'Oh, Jigsaw,' he sighed. 'Why couldn't you have made a film that has songs and dancing and lots and lots of great jokes like the ones Gary Gaggs tells? Who cares if no one likes it? Oh well.'

At the sound of the word 'songs', something mysterious began to happen. A little light on the computer began to blink. And then, with the words 'dancing' and 'jokes', there was more blinking and even a faint whirring sound.

'This computer's got a brain of its own,' Selby thought. 'I'd better do something before it deletes the movie.'

With this, Selby's paw slipped silently sideways, hitting the UPLOAD button.

Two hours later, Jigsaw Jabbar was woken by the sound of his mobile phone ringing.

'Hello?' he said sleepily. 'No, I feel great now, Harry. Sorry I got so cranky. I just needed a good sleep. And I'm sorry about the film. They what? They loved it? They said it's completely original? It isn't like anything they'd seen before? But hang on, Harry, I never sent the film. Are you sure? What's this about singing-

and-dancing battles scenes? And the princess telling jokes? I can't remember any of that. Oh, look, I didn't delete it, after all. It's still on my computer. I'll watch it right now and see what you're talking about. Where's that dog? No, a dog, Harry. There was a really nice dog in here — unless I dreamt him.'

For a second, Jigsaw Jabbar was sure he saw a tail disappear through the crack in the curtain. But then he looked again and wasn't so sure.

It was a smiling self-satisfied dog that slipped out through the back window of the theatre and into the cool night air.

'That's what I call a good night's work,' Selby thought as he headed for home.

THE STORY OF A STORY

The Funny Little Bunny

Once upon a time, a funny little bunny lived in a funny little bunny house with her happy little bunny brothers and sisters. Everything there was just happy happy happy all day long every day. Then one day the funny little bunny looked out the window.

'Why bless my funny little bunny tail,' she said. 'Here comes a storm . . .'

Melanie Mildew kept reading right to the end of her story.

But the naughty storm didn't knock the funny little bunny house down, so the funny little bunny and her little bunny brothers and sisters lived happily every after.

'What do you think?' she asked. 'Do you think it can win the Story Week story–writing competition?'

'Well, it is quite sweet,' Mrs Trifle said.

'Are you kidding? It's rubbish,' Aunt Jetty said. 'Kids don't want to hear about funny little bunnies. Listen to my one:

Space Monsters From Hell Get Blown to Bits

Ten-year-old Todd's Space-Buster rocket zoomed down to the planet Zikash-Splash Alpha 32. And then lots of three-headed monsters came out of holes in the ground. And then Todd turned his Duffertrog 309 Monster Blaster on them.

Blam! Blam! Blam!

'Kill kill kill!' he screamed.

And then the monsters exploded and green gunk went everywhere and even splattered Todd's Space-Buster rocket so he had to turn on the windscreen wipers.

Blamity boom! Blamity boom! Ker-blam! Ker-blam! Ker-blam!

Aunt Jetty went on and on to the end.

'Now that's a story!' she said. 'And I reckon it'll win.'

'Don't you think it's a bit violent?' Mrs Trifle asked.

'Of course it's violent. Kids love violence. Willy and Billy helped me write it and they're kids. Now it's your turn, Sis. Let's see if you can beat that.'

Mrs Trifle turned pink with embarrassment.

'I'm afraid I haven't written a word,' she said.

'But you can't just dip out,' Aunt Jetty said. 'This whole story-writing thing was your idea. You wanted everyone to go in it and see if we could win the prize money for the school library.'

'I just don't know what to write about.'

'Why not? You even took a writing course.'

'That was years ago and it was just to help me write reports for the Council. Making up stories is completely different.'

'I do think it's only fair that you write something, too,' Melanie Mildew said. 'I'll be back tomorrow to see how you've gone.'

★ ★ ★

That afternoon, Selby watched Mrs Trifle scribble on pieces of paper and then throw them all away. From time to time, she pulled her hair and sighed and moaned the way writers sometimes do when they can't think of what to write.

'Poor Mrs Trifle,' Selby thought. 'She can't write a story because she can't make things up. She's too honest.'

Mrs Trifle scrunched up another piece of paper.

'I give up,' she sighed.

'This is terrible!' Selby thought. 'I've got to help her, but how can I?'

Suddenly an idea-light went on in Selby's head.

'Hold the show! Where's that how-to-write book from her writing course? It's got to be around here somewhere.'

Selby raced to the bookcase and found the book. It was called *Writing for Ninnies*.

'I'm sure there was a chapter on story writing,' he thought, as he pawed through the pages. 'Yes! Here it is! Let's see now — *Story Starters*.'

Look around you. There are stories lurking everywhere, just waiting to be discovered. Look at your pants. Now use your imagination. What if they were on fire? How did the fire start? What's going to happen? There is the start of a story. Or look out the window. It's summer and it's hot. Now use your imagination. What if it suddenly turned cold and started snowing. There's a story in that, too. Or look at your husband or wife. What if they weren't who you thought they were? What if their body had been taken over by an alien. There's the start of another story.

'This is just what Mrs Trifle needs to get her started,' Selby thought. 'I'll just leave the book lying open on the floor.'

It wasn't long before Mrs Trifle noticed the book and picked it up.

'My old book. I forgot that I even had it. It must have fallen off the shelf,' Mrs Trifle said. 'And what a coincidence. It's opened to a page on story writing. Hmmm. *Look at your pants.*' Mrs Trifle looked down at her pants. '*What if they were on fire?* Well, they're not. Pants on fire. That's just silly. How would you make a story out of that?'

'There are lots of ways,' Selby thought. 'What if someone told a lie and the old *liar, liar pants on fire* rhyme came true?'

'*Look out the window,*' Mrs Trifle went on. '*It's summer and it's hot.* No, it's not. It's winter. *What if it suddenly turned cold and started snowing?* Well, it wouldn't surprise me.'

'It would me,' Selby sighed silently in his brain. 'Because it's never snowed in Bogusville before. But who cares? Just make something up! Think! What if a volcano came right up under Bogusville?'

'*Look at your husband or wife,*' Mrs Trifle read on. 'Well I don't have a wife and I can't look at my husband because he isn't here. All I can write about is what I do. And being the mayor of Bogusville isn't interesting enough for a story.'

'If only she could let her imagination run wild,' Selby thought. 'Why doesn't she imagine that she's not just the mayor of Bogusville but the mayor of . . . of the *universe*? Hey, I like it. Maybe I'll write it myself.'

That night, when the Trifles were sound

asleep, Selby went to the computer and answered some emails from kids.

'Now for my story,' he thought. 'What will I call it? How about *Mrs Trifle, Mayor of the Universe*. Okay, there's this evil dude from a different dimension who's trying get her sacked ...'

Selby's mind was racing ahead when he heard the sound of the toilet flushing.

'Uh-oh!' he thought. 'Someone's out of bed! They'll catch me using the computer! My secret will be out!'

Selby quickly turned off the computer and dived for the light switch. By the time Mrs Trifle looked into the study, Selby was lying innocently on the floor, pretending to sleep.

'Something very odd happened last night,' Mrs Trifle said at breakfast the next morning.

'Oh, yes? What was it?' Dr Trifle asked without looking up from his newspaper.

'Selby was in the study using the computer.'

'Gulp,' Selby gulped. 'I've finally been sprung!'

Dr Trifle put his newspaper down.

'Selby was using the computer?' he exclaimed. 'Are you kidding?!'

Mrs Trifle laughed.

'That got your attention,' she said. 'Yes, of course I'm kidding. I got up in the night and I thought I saw the light in the study go off. When I looked in, Selby was asleep on the floor.'

'You probably weren't completely awake,' Dr Trifle said. 'You imagined it.'

'I agree but it was great because it started me thinking about a story I want to write. I thought, what if Selby actually could understand what we say? What if he could read, write, speak and even use a computer?'

'Willy and Billy think that he *can* talk,' Dr Trifle said.

'I know, but you can't believe a word they say. Anyway, I'm going to write a story for Story Week about a dog that can talk.'

'I'm not sure I like this,' Selby thought. 'It's a little too close to the story of you-know-who.'

'Will this dog of yours talk to his owners?' Dr Trifle asked.

'No, it'll be a better story if he's trying to keep it a secret.'

'Why on earth would he want to do that? Will you make his owners nice people?'

'Of course. They'll be ... sort of like us. I've thought about this. I think the dog is keeping his talking a secret from his owners because he doesn't want to have to help out around the house,' Mrs Trifle said, looking over at Selby.

'She's making me feel guilty,' Selby thought.

'This sounds like those books about that talking dog,' Dr Trifle said. 'What's his name? Selby 🐾, that's it.'

'I keep forgetting about those books,' Mrs Trifle said.

'And remember the Search for Selby Society 🐾🐾 and how they were trying to find him?'

'How could I ever forget that,' Selby thought.

'Oh yes, I remember,' Mrs Trifle said. 'Well, I'm not going to call the dog in my story Selby.

🐾 *Paw note: Yes, he did say 'Selby', but remember that my real name isn't Selby.*

🐾🐾 *Paw note: See the story 'The Search for Selby'*
in this book.

S

I'll name him after our own dear Selby 🐾 instead.'

'This is getting worse by the minute!' Selby thought.

'That's funny,' Dr Trifle said. 'While you were talking, Selby's ears were up as if he was listening to us. Look, now they're not.'

'Can't a dog do anything around here any more?' Selby thought.

'There have been times when I've wondered about Selby,' Mrs Trifle said.

'Me too,' said Dr Trifle. 'Think of all the times we've come home and found the TV on and Selby lying there sleeping.'

'Or maybe just *pretending* to sleep,' Mrs Trifle said.

'How could you tell if he's pretending?'

'I could never be sure but when he's really sleeping he often has nightmares. And, when he does, his legs twitch and he makes those little *yip* and *yelp* sounds.'

'Okay, so now I guess I'm going to have to

🐾 Paw note: This time she used my real name but of course I can't tell you what it is. (Sorry.)

S

yip and yelp and twitch when I'm pretending to sleep,' Selby thought.

Mrs Trifle went on. 'Remember that time when we came home and he had his paws up against the fridge?'

'Yes, I do. We decided that he was probably just stretching but it really looked like he'd just closed the fridge door.'

'And he had cake crumbs on his chin,' Mrs Trifle added. 'Of course, he probably licked them up off the floor but, come to think of it, I've never actually seen him lick anything off the floor.'

'Oh boy,' Selby thought. 'Now I'm going to have to start licking the floor. Yuck! How would *they* like to lick the floor?'

'He doesn't lick himself, either,' Dr Trifle said. 'I thought all dogs cleaned their fur by licking themselves.'

'Oh, gross,' Selby thought.

'And yet he's always quite clean,' Mrs Trifle said. 'Remember the time there was water on the floor of the bathroom and you said, "I think Selby just had a shower?"'

'Yes,' Dr Trifle laughed. 'That was funny.'

'You know, I've never seen Selby lick his nose when it's runny the way other dogs do,' Mrs Trifle said.

'Now that ...' Selby thought, 'that is where I draw the line. There's no way I'm going to lick my nose. I don't think my tongue is long enough, anyway.'

'And I've never ever seen him drink out of a toilet the way Aunt Jetty's dog, Crusher, used to.'

'Hold the show!' Selby thought. 'Forget about that other line! This is where I really draw the line! There's no way I'd ever drink out of a toilet! I'd rather die of thirst.'

For the next few days, Mrs Trifle watched Selby's every move and made notes for her story.

'This is awful!' Selby thought. 'I have to be soooo careful! I'm missing all my fave TV shows, I'm only eating Dry-Mouth Dog Biscuits, I have to *yip* and *yelp* and twitch when I'm pretending to sleep, and I've licked so much floor that my tongue is ready to fall off. Why did I ever try to help Mrs Trifle with her story writing?'

The days went on with Selby more and more exhausted from having to be completely doglike. He even brought a stick to Mrs Trifle and stood in front of her, jumping back and forth till she threw it.

'I hate chasing sticks,' he thought. 'My life is a catastrophe! How long do I have to keep this dog-stuff up? I have to be soooo careful. I just wish she'd finish her story and I could go back to normal.'

Gradually, Mrs Trifle began to lose interest.

'My story is getting to be just like the stories about Selby,' she told Dr Trifle. 'The more I write, the more Selby seems like Selby in the books. I don't want my story to be too much like them. It'll seem like I'm copying.'

And, just when she was about to give up and let Selby get back to his normal life, it happened. Selby was lying next to the TV licking his paw for the twentieth time and daydreaming when Dr Trifle accidentally stepped on his tail.

'*Ouch*!' Selby cried.

'Ouch?' Dr Trifle said. 'Did he just say *ouch*?'

'*Yelp! Yelp! Yelp!*' Selby cried. '*Yip! Yip! Yip!*'

'It sounded like *ouch* to me, too,' Mrs Trifle said, 'but maybe not. You know, I've been thinking. What if he actually *is* the dog in the books?'

'Whatever do you mean?'

'What if Selby can talk and read and write and all those things and he's the one who rings up Duncan Ball and tells him his stories and Duncan just writes them down?'

'You mean that dog might actually be a *real* dog?'

'Yes, *our* dog, our own dear Selby,' Mrs Trifle said. 'The signs have been there all the time, just like the Search for Selby Society people said.'

'You're serious, aren't you?'

'Absolutely. Let's just say that Selby had opened the fridge that time. And let's just say that he did turn the lights on when we were out and that he even watches TV. Let's just say that he does use the computer when we're asleep. We keep making excuses for him.'

'I see what you mean,' Dr Trifle said slowly.

They both turned and looked Selby in the eye.

'Okay, Selby, time's up,' Mrs Trifle said. 'Talk to us.'

'Yes, Selby,' Dr Trifle said, 'enough is enough. Let's put a stop to this nonsense right now.'

Selby looked back and forth from one to the other.

'I'm going to have to do it,' he thought. 'I've got to finally put their minds at ease. This is it.'

Selby got to his feet. He cleared his throat and licked his lips. Dr and Mrs Trifle stared in disbelief.

'What do you think he's about to do?' asked Mrs Trifle.

'He's ... he's going to the loo,' Dr Trifle said as he watched Selby trot down the hallway. '*Our* loo.'

Selby put his head down into the toilet bowl. Tears flooded his eyes.

'I'm going to have to step over that line,' he thought, 'and drink out of the toilet. I've got to do it to convince the Trifles that I'm just an ordinary toilet-drinking dog. Oh woe woe woe! Look at that awful, smelly, disgusting mess. The loo looks like it hasn't been cleaned for weeks. I'll probably die of some terrible toilet disease! I can't do it! But I *have* to do it! Here goes ...'

Dr and Mrs Trifle could hear the sound of little splashes from where they sat in the loungeroom.

'Good grief!' Mrs Trifle cried. 'Selby is actually drinking out of the toilet!'

'I do believe you're right,' Dr Trifle agreed. 'Do you think the real Selby, the dog in the books, would drink out of a toilet?'

'I don't think so,' Mrs Trifle said. 'He's too ...

too *human*. That would be like one of us drinking out of the loo.'

'So that settles it,' Dr Trifle said. 'Selby can't be the dog in the books, after all.'

'You're absolutely right,' Mrs Trifle agreed. 'And I'd better stop him from drinking out of the toilet right now before he catches some terrible toilet disease.'

Mrs Trifle got to the bathroom just in time not to see Selby as he slipped the toilet brush back into its holder, and just in time to see him about to take his first slurp.

'Selby! Stop that!' Mrs Trifle cried, picking him up in her arms. 'Oh, you poor poor dear. Come away from there and let me fill your drinking bowl with clean, fresh water.'

'Phew! That was a close one,' Selby thought. 'Saved by the brush.'

This isn't the end. Mrs Trifle did finally write her story but it wasn't about Selby. It was about something she knew quite a bit about — being a mayor.

When Dr Trifle asked her where the idea came from she said: 'I can't remember. I was looking at my notes on the computer and there was this title there — 'Mrs Trifle, Mayor of the Universe'. I forgot I'd even written it down. But it got me thinking.'

So that was the story Mrs Trifle finally wrote and it even won the competition. Everyone loved it, especially Selby.

SELBY
SHATTERED

Selby struggled around the room, getting slower and slower. He could barely lift his paws or move his legs.

'I've got to keep moving!' he screamed in his brain. 'If I stop, I'll never be able to move again!'

The Trifles watched in horror as Selby stood up on his hind legs, stretched his front paws upwards, and then came to a stop.

'Selby, what's wrong?' Mrs Trifle cried, clutching him in her arms. 'You're as hard as a rock!'

'I'm frozen!' Selby screamed. 'And it's all Dr Trifle's fault! He poisoned me!'

Or at least that's what he tried to scream but by then it was too late. He couldn't move his lips or his tongue or even his vocal cords. The only sound that came out of him was a tiny rush of air.

And then his lungs stopped working.

And his heart stopped.

'This is awful!' Mrs Trifle cried, as the tears poured down her face. 'This is terrible! It's a tragedy! How could this have happened to him?'

It all started earlier that day. Mrs Trifle had just come home from work as Dr Trifle came out of his workroom.

'Boy, is it hot today!' Mrs Trifle said, getting a jug of cold water from the fridge. 'I just wish summer would finally end.'

'She can say that again,' Selby thought as he slurped some cool water from his bowl. 'And I'm twice as hot because I'm covered in fur.'

'Stop!' Dr Trifle called out. 'You'd better not drink that.'

Mrs Trifle looked at the scribbled label on the pitcher.

'*Do not drink!*' she read out loud. 'Why? What's wrong with it? It's just cold water, isn't it?'

'Yes, it is cold water but it's not *normal* cold water,' Dr Trifle replied. 'It's a new kind of water that I invented.'

'You invented a new kind of water?'

'I did. Pour some into your glass. I'll show you something.'

Mrs Trifle poured some of the water into a glass.

'Now, just leave it for a moment to let it warm up.'

After a couple of minutes, Dr Trifle said, 'Now turn the glass upside-down.'

'But it'll go all over the floor,' Mrs Trifle protested.

'No it won't.'

Mrs Trifle slowly turned the glass upside-down but the water stayed in the bottom.

'It's gone all hard — like ice,' she said.

'It's Nice,' Dr Trifle said proudly.

'Well, yes, it's very nice but — '

'No, no,' Dr Trifle interrupted. 'It's *Nice* with a capital N. It's short for *not ice*. Nice. Get it? That's my name for it. It freezes when it warms up instead of freezing when it gets cold. What you have in that glass is a Nice block.'

'A Nice block? How did you discover this Nice?'

'Sort of by accident. I was heating some water to make a cup of tea. Then I changed my mind. It was too hot to drink tea. I thought, why not make some iced tea? That started me thinking about what would happen if you heated and cooled water at the same time.'

'It did?'

'Yes. So I put the water-heater thingy in the freezer and, well, somehow it changed normal water into Nice water. When I poured it into my tea cup, it warmed up and froze solid.'

'I never did understand about water freezing,' Mrs Trifle said. 'At school they told us that water was made of little bits like soldiers running around everywhere. When you made it really cold, the soldiers lined up in rows and then they all held hands like one solid block.'

'Soldiers? Holding hands?' Dr Trifle said. 'I'll have to think about that.'

Suddenly the Nice fell from Mrs Trifle's upside-down glass and smashed on the floor.

'Oops!' Mrs Trifle said.

Dr Trifle put the jug of Nice water back in the fridge.

'Hmm, that's strange,' he said. 'I could have sworn there was more than this. I wonder what happened to the rest of it.'

'Oh no!' Selby thought as his tongue suddenly struck something hard in his bowl. 'I've just been drinking it! I filled my bowl from that jug in the fridge!'

Selby struggled around the room, getting slower and slower. He could barely lift his paws or move his legs.

'I've got to keep moving!' he screamed in his brain.

(All of which brings us back to where we were at the beginning.)

'I think he must have drunk some of the Nice water,' Dr Trifle said, touching the hard water in Selby's bowl.

'Did you give it to him?'

'No. At least, I don't think I did.'

'But you must have. He couldn't have got the jug out of the fridge all by himself, poured some in his bowl and then put it back. Call the vet! Quick!'

155

Minutes later, the vet arrived.

'What's that?' he exclaimed, pointing to Selby.

'That's Selby, our darling, wonderful dog. He's gone all ... all solid. It's too complicated to explain. Can you unstiffen him?'

The man listened to Selby's chest. 'I think he's gone.'

'What do you mean, gone?' Selby thought. 'I'm right here!'

'What do you mean, gone?' Mrs Trifle asked.

'We vets have a special word for it. The word is *dead*. I'm terribly sorry,' the man said, looking at his watch, 'Oops, I've got another appointment.'

'No! No! No!' Mrs Trifle cried. 'Oh, Selby, my dearest, darling dog!'

'We love you, Selby,' wailed Dr Trifle. 'You can't be dead!'

'I'm not dead!' Selby thought. 'Okay, so I can't move but I'm not dead!'

'What are we going to do?' Mrs Trifle cried. 'He was the most darling dog you could ever imagine.'

'I was and I am,' Selby thought.

'He was just so lovable,' Dr Trifle whimpered.

'I still am!' Selby thought. 'Just thaw me out and I'll be even more lovable.'

And so it was that Selby was stuck frozen to the spot, standing on his hind legs in the loungeroom. The Trifles sat on the couch with tears in their eyes, not knowing what to do with their beloved pet.

'I can tell you what to do with him,' Aunt Jetty said when she called around. 'Put him out with the rubbish before he starts to stink. Come to think of it, he already stinks.'

'What an awful thing to say!' Mrs Trifle sobbed. 'I can't believe you said that!'

'I was only trying to help.'

Dr Trifle tried everything he could to melt Selby. He put him in the bathtub and filled it with ice — real ice. Selby thought he'd die of cold. Then, after he'd dried him off again, Dr Trifle put a dozen electric blankets around him and turned them on.

'He's going to cook me!' Selby thought. 'But maybe this'll work, after all.'

But it didn't.

'I guess the soldiers are still holding hands,' Mrs Trifle sighed. 'If only there was something we could do to make them let go.'

But there wasn't. It seemed that once water turned to Nice there was no going back.

Dr Trifle rang all his science and inventor friends who tried everything they could think of to melt Selby. They zapped him with electricity and they jiggled him and they even tickled him.

'We've never seen anything like it,' they said. 'The strange thing is that his brain scan is still showing multi-morphic auto-synchronicity between the frontal and backal lobes. It's as if his brain's still working. But of course that's not possible.'

Crowds of people came from all over Bogusville, Poshfield and then from every corner of Australia and, perhaps, the world to see The Frozen Dog.

Newspaper people wrote stories about him and TV news people stood in front of him, talking about him, while their cameras buzzed and whirred.

'I hate this!' Selby thought. 'For years I kept my secret a secret because I didn't want to be studied by scientists. And I didn't want everybody coming around and bugging me. Now it's all happening and I can't even run away and hide! Oh, woe woe woe. The only thing that hasn't happened to me yet is being dognapped!'

(Funny he should say that because that very night Mrs Trifle chased away some robbers who had come to steal him.)

'We have to do something,' Mrs Trifle said. 'We can't go on like this. I think we'll have to send him away. We can't have him in the house any more. I just can't stand it.'

'But where would we send him?'

Dr Trifle's old friend Professor Krakpott had the answer.

'Put him on display,' he said, 'in the Museum of Old and Crusty Things.'

And so began the second part of Selby's frozen life. He stood in the middle of the museum surrounded by dinosaur bones and lots of other old museum stuff.

Days went by and then weeks and months. And, just when it seemed like everyone in the world had seen The Amazing Frozen Dog, more people came.

'I can't sleep,' Selby whimpered in his brain. 'I can't even close my eyes. This is the worst thing that could ever happen to a dog — or a person.'

But, deep in Selby's little non-beating heart, he knew that when things were really really bad suddenly everything could change. And he was right — things got worse.

It was on a weekday and lots of school groups had been to the museum to see him. It was when the girls of St Lucre's School for Polite Young Ladies came through the museum that Selby knew his problems were really starting.

Among the group were Mrs Trifle's uncle's cousin's brother-in-law's stepson's daughters, Cindy, Mindy and Lindy 🐾. Selby spied them out of the corner of his eye.

'Oh, no, not them again,' Selby thought, as the line of little girls in their cleanest, neatest school uniforms filed by.

'Hey, look. It's that awful Trifle dog,' Cindy whispered.

'Frozen stiff,' Mindy giggled.

'Let's have some fun,' Lindy said.

'Oh no!' Selby thought. 'They're up to no good. Though how could they make things worse than they already are?'

🐾 Paw note: If you haven't already read the story called 'Selby Meets the Triple Terror' in this book, maybe you should do so right now.   S

161

Soon, all the other girls had filed by and the terrible tripets were left alone.

'I know,' Cindy said, pulling a big bone from a dinosaur skeleton.

'Good thinking,' Mindy said, grabbing another bone.

'One, two, and ...' Lindy said, swinging another dinosaur bone, '... three!'

The first blow hit Selby on the back with a *smack*!

The next blow was to his side. *Thwack*!

And the third blow went right to his middle. *Crack*!

Selby stood there for a moment with cracks all over him. Then, in one big crash, he shattered into hundreds of pieces and landed on the floor.

A guard came running.

'What happened?!' he yelled. 'Who did this?'

'I don't know,' Cindy said sweetly.

'We didn't see a thing,' Mindy said, twirling her hair with one finger.

'He just cracked, that's all,' Lindy said.

'You don't think *we* did it, do you?' the girls all said together in their sweetest voices.

'Of course not,' the guard said. 'Hurry along now, girls.'

And so it was that Selby lay shattered on the floor in bits and pieces like Humpty Dumpty.

His head was still in one piece and he watched helplessly as Professor Krakpott and his helpers went to work on him. But all the museum's scientists and all the museum's men couldn't put Selby together again.

'Well, I guess that's the end of him,' the professor said, starting to sweep up the pieces of Selby.

That would have been the end except one last person happened along. And that person was famous film-maker and expert jigsaw puzzler Jigsaw Jabbar 🐾. And there was nothing that excited Jigsaw more than a puzzle.

'What are you doing?' Dr Krakpott cried.

'Stand back, everyone,' Jigsaw said, 'there's a puzzle to be solved.'

🐾 *Paw note: Remember him from 'The Movie Magic of Jigsaw Jabbar'?*

S

He picked up two pieces of Selby and put them together. His quick eyes scanned the floor and he picked up another and joined that to the others.

'I can't believe it!' Professor Krakpott said.

Piece by tiny piece, Jigsaw put Selby back together again. He got bigger and bigger and bigger until finally Jigsaw lifted Selby's head onto his body.

'I can't believe it,' Selby thought. 'I'm back together again and I'm not falling apart. Goodness me, I can move my toes! I can move my legs. I can bend! The soldiers aren't holding hands any more! The Nice has melted! It's a miracle! The guy is a genius!'

'This dog looks familiar,' Jigsaw said. 'Hmmm, I wonder where I've seen him before.'

It was a very happy and un-frozen dog who was taken back to his home in Bogusville.

'Selby! Oh, Selby! You're here!' Mrs Trifle cried. 'You darling dog!'

'Yes,' Dr Trifle said, 'you are the most wonderful dog there ever was.'

'And you two,' Selby thought as he blinked back a tear, 'are the dearest, most wonderful people in the whole world.'

'And yet two fellow thought that he blessed badness that are the cleanest, most wonderful people in the whole world.

GARY GAGGS' HECKLER BUSTERS

When hecklers interrupt Gary Gaggs' comedy shows, he has lots of what he calls 'heckler busters' to make fun of them and get them to stop. Here are some good ones:

- 'I never forget a face but in your case I'll try.'

- 'Oh my goodness! Look at your face! Was anyone else hurt in the accident?'

- 'This guy is descended from royalty. His grandfather was King Kong.'

166

🐾 'Thanks for your point of view. Come to think of it, it matches the point on your head.'

🐾 'But seriously, folks, this guy tried to leave his brain to science but they rejected it.'

🐾 'I'm not saying that he's dumb but mind-readers only charge him half price.'

🐾 'So you think you're a wit? Well at least you're *half* right.'

'You've got a lot of well-wishers here. These people wish they could throw you down a well.'

'Excuse me, sir, but did you get up bright and early this morning, or just early?'

'You may not know it but you just won the lucky door prize. Will someone please show him the door?'

'Your mother must have been a weight-lifter to raise a dumbbell like you.'

'This guy isn't bald, he's just taller than his hair. It's not a great head but I'm sure he'd never part with it.'

'When he was at school he got nothing but underwater marks. They were all below C level.'

'He had to leave school because of illness and fatigue. The principal got sick and tired of him.'

TAIL

Well, now that you've reached the **tail** end of these **tales**, what do you think? Weren't Cindy, Mindy and Lindy little shockers?! They make Willy and Billy seem like saints. And wasn't it terrible about that Nice that Dr Trifle invented? I loved Gary Gagge' 'Hopeless Little Brother' jokes, but whoever would have thought that... Ooops! I'd better not say too much in case you might be reading this **tail**-end bit before you read the **tales** themselves.

Anyway, I hope you liked this book. And I hope there'll be more **tales** about me, but, with the SSS (The Search for Selby Society) people after me, I don't know what's going to happen next!

CYA,

 Selby

ABOUT THE AUTHOR

Duncan Ball is an Australian author and scriptwriter, who writes popular books for children. This book, *Selby Shattered*, is the fourteenth story collection about Selby, 'the only talking dog in Australia and, perhaps, the world'. There is also a collection of Selby stories taken from the other books called *Selby's Selection*, and two jokes books: *Selby's Joke Book* and *Selby's Side-Splitting Joke Book*.

Duncan has also written the Emily Eyefinger books, a series about the adventures of a girl who was born with an eye on the end of her finger, and the comedy novels *Piggott Place* and *Piggotts in Peril* about the frustrations of a twelve-year-old boy, Bert Piggott, in a never-ending struggle to get his family of ratbags and dreamers out of trouble.

Duncan lives in Sydney with his wife, Jill, and their cat, Jasper. Duncan wanted to see if the Selby stories would be good bedtime stories so he read one to Jasper and, sure enough, Jasper slept right through it.

For more information about Duncan and his books, see Selby's site at:

www.harpercollins.com.au/selby

ACKNOWLEDGMENTS

Of all the people involved in the making of this book, the author would particularly like to thank Jill Quin, Shona Martyn, Lisa Berryman, Jo Butler, Cristina Cappelluto and Barbara Mobbs.

Selby, the only talking dog in Australia and, perhaps, the world, is in a bit of a mess. So much of a mess, in fact, that you might call it a shemozzle!

Selby's shemozzle starts when he tells a joke that's so funny, he puts the whole town of Bogusville in the hospital. And he doesn't stop there …

Between being coated in chocolate and almost eaten by those horrible brats, Willy and Billy, falling in love with the world's first talking cat, pretending to be a seeing-eye dog and maybe — just maybe — changing the recipe of Dry-Mouth Dog Biscuits, Selby is in a right shemozzle. But the biggest shemozzle of all is when he becomes invisible …

How does he get himself out of it?

Prepare to laugh yourself silly as you find out!